Clockwork

Purple

To Mary Ann,
Thank you for your support!
Happy Reading!. Aingeal Rose

Linda Kay

**Bend Creative Writers, Aingeal Rose O'Grady,
Charles Scamahorn, Dell Blackman,
Harriette Hoover Green,
Kevin O'Grady, Linda Kay**
https://clockworkpurple.com

Clockwork Purple Vol 1: A Collection of Short Stories.

Bend Creative Writers.
ISBN: 978-1-880765-01-2

Artwork: AHONU.com
Manuscript Designer & Layout: AHONU.com
Published by: Harmony House Books, an imprint of
Twin Flame Productions
Printed in the United States of America

Address all inquiries to:
Twin Flame Productions, LLC
358 SE Sena Court, Bend, OR 97702
+1-224-588-8026
admin@twinflameproductions.us
http://twinflameproductions.us

Clockwork

Purple

DEDICATION

This book reveals a smorgasbord of delight from such a small group of people. ~ Aingeal Rose

We dedicate this book to aspiring writers everywhere. To all those who suffer from writer's block, follow our lead here and you'll never suffer from it again!

We dedicate this book to random creativity. We found our creativity in random sentences, in random books from a random group of people.

When we started out, we never imagined our writings would become a book, but now that they have, we dedicate our book to all the books from where we got our inspiration.

And finally, we dedicate this book to you, our readers. While the kick from writing was exciting, having you read it is the real icing on the cake!

Creative BEND Writers

Fourth of July 2017 Bend, OR

PREFACE

ON a Monday morning in the summer of 2016, a small group of friends met to form a Creative Writing group on the second floor of Dudley's Bookshop Café in Bend, Oregon. Their method was to pick a *prompt* or sentence at random from one of the hundreds of books on the shelves, and then write spontaneously for 45-minutes. The only rule was that the prompt had to be used somewhere in their story exactly as it was phrased. At the end of the time, they would read their stories aloud to each other without fear of criticism. It soon became evident that the stories were not only entertaining, they were diverse, healing, thought-provoking, often comical, and certainly worthy of publishing!

As you feast your imagination on the stories, you'll find how each author has uniquely treated the prompt. Each story is a chapter, where each author contributes their interpretation of the same prompt, and for clarity and ease, the stories and the authors are in alphabetical order throughout.

Bend Creative Writers hope you will find fun, inspiration and healing in their first volume of short stories and that you will enjoy reading them as much as they have enjoyed writing them!

Table of Contents

Prompt #1

Clockwork Purple

AINGEAL ROSE O'GRADY

Time, for those in the know, is a fairytale. It is entirely made up by the minds of billions of people who believe in it. It is used to continue the linear way of thinking — past to present, to future. In essence, it assures a continuity, a progression of the species.

Gabriel had had enough. He felt his entire existence had been bound by time. He felt time was a prisoner. What can one look forward to — wasn't time an inevitable march to the grave? Isn't the tick-tock, tick-tock of the clock a constant reminder of where we'll all end up? And what about the stress hormones produced on the subconscious level while humanity waits and wonders when time will be up for them? Gabriel knew these were morbid thoughts, but he couldn't deny them. He wanted off the wheel of time — he wanted off the clock. Isn't this what karma was all about? Isn't this what the spiritual elite mean when they talk about getting off the wheel of karma, or the wheel of time?

It seems humanity, nature, plants and universes are all bound by time — called *cycles*.

The grand plan is one giant wheel — wheels within wheels. Life itself seemed timed. Astrology has its wheels and watches as we cycle through the zodiac over and over again. The Vedas have their wheels called *yuga's* that repeat, cycle, and repeat. Gabriel had studied these teachings and had always come to the same conclusion — time was a trap. Cycles were a trap. Motion was just one big torus of expansion and contraction with no end in sight — a repetitive motion of birth and death. No wonder history repeats itself with little or no actual evolution. We don't seem to get any closer to freedom from the wheel of time.

Gabriel felt life was a no-win situation. He termed his despondency *clockwork purple* — an apt description of his mood. Could he stop his own internal wheel, his own clock? What would it mean to do so? He had considered suicide, but he knew it would not end the cycle of time for him. The very idea of it only confirmed his belief in time. It would just continue the prison in his mind. There had to be another answer, what was it? And what would be the proof that he was free of time? He wanted to have control, to be the decider of his fate. Wasn't time also memory? Wasn't this what kept the linear mind plodding along — the memories built into the cellular structure of every living thing? Was memory what kept life alive, or was memory what made life die? What would happen if he could clear his body and mind from being the effect of memory?

If his body was made from memories, how would it change if he actively decided to erase them all? What if his cells were cleansed of all memories that caused it to age and die? Would he then end the cycle for himself? Is this what it means to be in the *present*? Can one stop the recording process within oneself? Where would a person arrive if they could do it? Would they arrive anywhere or would they cease to exist?

Gabriel once met a woman who had erased her memory time stream. She had gone back and erased her identification with all her previous lives, as well as her identification with her genetic lines. She ended up in an entirely different perception of reality. She felt she had come back to the truth of herself — a reality outside of time and cycles. Gabriel knew he had to try it. This could be the answer. For 90 days he did meditations that erased any memory or program within him that thwarted his highest good. He could feel the changes occurring within him — he felt lighter, happier and more loving. His mind was opening to higher information which would flow spontaneously and uninhibited into his mind. His attitude about time changed — he no longer felt trapped by it. It simply no longer mattered. Gabriel knew he was becoming free of it by letting go of his attachments to things associated with time and cycles.

And so it was that in 90 days he was a different man. He was on his way to becoming a master.

CHARLES SCAMAHORN

A blank of confusion has settled into my mind. I have nothing to say! I worry that my life is empty and meaningless and that my behavior is viewed by others as weird. Those strange thoughts are not me, not the real me, and I am not a clockwork and I am not purple. Those are external fantasies imposed through words by other people's expostulations vibrating in the air. That's not the reality of who I am.

I'm just a person interested in solving problems that face me and especially those problems that confront all humanity. I prefer to ponder problems where I can contribute a meaningful new idea into the current of human understanding. That is, I seek to add something significant to the vastness of human wisdom.

There is an infinity of problems to be found and I do mean infinity in the mathematical sense of the word; the infinite vastness beyond the current human situation and comprehension.

There is an infinity of undiscovered problems beyond those met by the hundred billion people who have lived on this Earth.

There are, without a doubt, problems that could be discovered and revealed now with a simple declarative statement. Undoubtedly a sentence, a phrase, even a few words could be said at this moment that would change humanity forever. For example, a common simple phrase known now by nearly everyone was unknown by anyone two-hundred years ago. It changed the world. There are many other examples, but the phrase *survival of the fittest* has had a major impact on all humanity.

That idea was obvious even to Adam Smith in his book *Wealth of Nations*, published in 1776, some eight decades before Darwin published *The Origin of Species* in 1859, but Smith didn't understand the concept's broader applications and limited his idea to a *hidden hand* that brings about the survival of the fittest in business. Darwin et al. expanded the concept to biologically adaptive things and not just to business. Darwin's phrase had a much broader application and vastly greater impact than Smith's.

There are in all likelihood many ideas and phrases as powerful as *survival of the fittest* that could be stated right now by you; but they haven't been said, at least not said in a way that reached the public and *went viral*. Those are the ideas I like to search for and the strange places I like to seek out and explore.

It is a simple thing to be doing, and it seems like everyone is doing it every moment of their lives.

So... Why am I said to be weird? I dress in clothing that isn't particularly different. I speak with common English words. My grammar is apparently understandable to the people I meet. From the feedback I get from others it appears the thoughts I express are generally understood. I try diligently to obey all laws and never lie. So, I ask again... Why am I considered weird?

The prompt *Clockwork Purple* is a simple English phrase. The word *purple* refers to a common color and is a common word. The word *clockwork* is a bit unusual, but it's an easy compound of two very common words and is easily understood. In our writer's group, the usage implies a clock in our background guiding the timing of our work and encouraging prompt productivity. And, the word *purple* is commonly associated with florid spontaneous writing. Thus, the title for our book *Clockwork Purple* is descriptive as well as colorful, and it implies the exploration of the outer realms of our present reality.

Our title, *Clockwork Purple*, implies weird, but it also implies prompt, important, colorful and royal.

HARRIETTE HOOVER GREEN

Tick, tick, tick went the old grandfather clock in the library. *Oh, I must hurry, I'm late again!* She rushed around gathering her necessities for the meeting; her papers, gloves, purse, hat and coat.

Once in the carriage she let out a large exhale of breath. Her mind was racing to run through the list of tasks and topics to cover in the meeting. The task seemed too big to tackle at one time, but one time is all she had to complete it. Would they be willing to even listen to her thoughts and proposals for the property? The Trust clearly explained the intended use for the community, but that does not mean that their idea of community use is the only use. She must make them see her vision, she must!

As she rode along, she listened to the clop, clop, clop of the horses hooves. It became a calming, rhythmic lulling in her body, and slowly she relaxed.

It will be what it will be.

That thought calmed her and provided a sense of wellbeing, filling her entire body, allowing her muscles to relax. She had survived the loss of her entire family, which was resurrected by this recent death of her grandfather — all the sadness and pain flooding back.

Clockwork Purple, what does that mean? What did her grandfather want her to do by using that phrase in the Trust? Clockwork, clockwork, does that mean use your time efficiently? Or, always be aware of the timing of things? Or, work by the clock? It was a mystery she did not solve before the Board of Trustees decided they needed to meet and discuss the disbursement of the Trust funds. Whenever she thought those words, her mind would swirl in a purple haze, like drowning in a purple-black sea, the clock ticking away. Dying is hard work, especially drowning. One's mind must realize you only have a few minutes to live before you stop struggling and sink into the purple-black water as the time keeps moving forward. The clock will continue to tick even after your awareness is gone. Tick-tock, tick-tock.

As her mind turned the phrase over and over, the sound of the horse's hooves formed a perfect rhythm, almost hypnotizing her.

In her mind's eye she saw the color purple flood her brain, forming a beautiful back drop for the vision of a giant clock, tick, tick, tick.

She had been grieving the loss of her grandfather's death, occurring while she was on her honeymoon. She went from euphoria to devastation in one instant. The solicitor telephoned the hotel in Africa where she and her new husband were staying and broke the news. She was stunned and numb with no thoughts at all. She did not cry, she did not wail, she did not scream, she stood silent.

Grandfather had raised her alone after her entire family was killed when the *unsinkable* Titanic sank. The thoughts of how they died was so horrific she would close her mind down instantly whenever their deaths were mentioned. The fact that she was not able to take the trip with them because she contracted the hard measles and was in isolation to prevent the ailment from spreading, as was the practice at that time, was just a matter of chance. Grandfather was her only living family, and now he was gone. She felt desperately alone in the world.

Clockwork Purple brought forth the image of a purple clock with golden numbers. The color purple had always been her favorite color and grandfather knew that.

He would bring home purple dresses in every shade, purple flowers, hats, shoes and jewelry. She knew he loved her greatly and only wanted her happiness, not insisting on her going away to school or finding an appropriate husband. He was content to have her at home with him, almost like he was afraid that if she were out of sight she would disappear. He also missed her mother, Ailene, and Isabella's siblings.

It was all too tragic.

She shifted her mind back to the dilemma of the meeting and her intention to ask the Board to build a large swimming pool for the community on the property grandfather left to her in the Trust, along with sufficient funds to support the building and maintenance of the pool, as well as the huge house and grounds. Her needs were covered in the Trust as well.

Her vision of the term Clockwork Purple was for a place that ordinary people and their families could come to learn to swim.

Wait, I know, I know what he was saying! she thought. He too saw the pool as a life saving opportunity for the entire community. He, who insisted she take swimming lessons immediately after the funeral of her family. He too, saw the connection with the purple-black water in the pool and the ticking of the clock of life, moving forward.

The problem was in using their beautiful, luscious property for the public to come. There would be people up close on the private property. It might feel like an invasion. But, it may well save lives. *The Board must see the value,* she thought. They all knew the family's tragic story. They had compassion, she would make them see her vision. There could be a natural barrier of trees between the pool and the house. They would find a way, they would find a way, she knew it.

"What on earth is that?" Rose exclaimed. The shimmering light from the orb was purple with some indigo, pink and violet flames, and there were twelve striations of light that radiated out from the center like a clock-face.

"I don't know," Evan replied, "it's weird. It's like a UFO of some kind."

"You're right, it is weird. Let's get out of here!" Rose said. "I've seen this before and it's not good." Rose was recalling a memory from when she was twelve years old. She was lying on her bed in tears. She thought the purple clock she had just seen was a sort of coming of age, a sort of recognition that she was now in full puberty. But then the orb had descended down on top of her, completely enveloping her. She felt it enter every cell of her body. She became absorbed by the light, so much so that she felt she was inside it, and it was inside her.

Then the orb raised her up and she started to drift up toward the ceiling and magically morph through the roof so she could see the night sky above her. She remembered it felt good, but then a single thought frightened her. How will I be able to get back? With that thought she was immediately back on her bed.

Not wanting to know the details, Evan felt her fear first, then his own childhood terrors started to rise inside him. He grabbed her by the hand and started running from their favorite spot on Lovers Lane towards the lake. But the orb followed them, they in panic, while the orb just glided along with ease and grace. No matter how fast they ran the purple light just stayed gently hovering over them.

Exhausted, they flopped down on the soft sand beside their rock on the lakeshore. It was a bright moonlit night and the moon reflected slivers of silver light onto the shimmering water. Their names inside a heart was painted perfectly on the rock in white poster paint they had one day taken from their art class. With nowhere to go, they simultaneously reconciled themselves to the worst.

"We'll go together," whispered Evan. "It is what we always wanted, isn't it?" Not sure if he was ready to hear Rose's answer, he immediately blurted out, "I love you!"

"I love you, too," she whispered back, a little hesitantly. "Hold me!"

The orb hovered over them like a low cloud. They could almost touch it, but dared not. All they could do was stare, their bodies frozen like statues fallen to the sand. The striations from the center of the orb radiated out and started spinning, slowly at first, then faster and faster. They could hear a low hum at first, growing to a high-pitched whine, then to a level where it almost went out of their hearing range. Rose could see numbers, lots of them, and they seemed to be randomly created. There were single digits and numbers with thousands of digits spinning dizzily over their heads.

Suddenly Rose recognized some numbers and the numbers were accompanied by scenes, events and even sound tones. She saw when she was six year old, then twelve, and then eighteen. She saw Evan at the same ages. Twelve and six are eighteen. Then she saw the year 6 AD, 600 AD, 1200 AD, 1800 AD and then the same years before Christ.

Evan was witnessing the same thing. He watched astonished as he realized they had been together in all those times. They watched themselves embrace in multiple scenes as if the orb was a gigantic movie screen set against the stars overhead.

Then they realized they could influence the sequence of events. When they thought, *slow down*, the virtual movie slowed down, and when they thought, *fast forward*, it would swirl to a new timeline marked evenly by multiples of twelve.

When his fear slowed to a point where he could rationalize what he was seeing, Evan mumbled, "Is that really us?"

"Yes, that's us, Evan. We have been together in other lifetimes. It is showing us all of them." Rose felt a reconciling of all her lost loves, a kind of forgiveness for all the pain and hurt she had gone through throughout her lives. She knew then this was something beautiful and was not to be feared.

Evan, however, was struggling. He was carrying denial from years of childhood abuse and from having to grow up too fast. He felt the fear of having to play the father-role before his time in too many lifetimes.

In an instant he relived the pain of rejection from others he loved, but every time he saw Rose, his pain turned to pure joy. He could feel the tears begin to roll down his cheeks as he recognized he was with the love of his life in all those lifetimes, and she was with him right here, right now. Rose was the one he always loved through all eternity. He turned away so she would not see his tears.

The purple clocklike orb stopped spinning and started to rise. "No," they both uttered in unison. "Let us see more." The orb obeyed instantly and came down again slowly until it was just above their bodies. They felt all the fear leave them, and in its place a gentle loving peace arose within them. It started in their stomachs and slowly radiated outward just like the orb. It filled every muscle, every bone, every fiber, every cell in their bodies until they were entirely immersed in it. Then they started to rise up into the center of the orb until they floated in the purple light.

"Oh no," Evan cried, "please!"

"It's okay," said Rose reassuringly. "It's okay. We can do it this time. I remember this now from before. I called it *Clockwork Purple* the last time. It has come back for us on our eighteenth birthday. It wants to tell us something. Here, hold my hand." She didn't realize that he was already holding her hand, but he had held it so tight that it was numb.

Slowly at first, they rose into the purple light. This time they knew not to have negative thoughts that might shock them back to the cold sand on the moonlit lakeshore. Instead, they reconciled themselves to their future, whatever that might be.

The day reflected the mood of the mourners; dreary, rainy and cold. The small group huddled under the sparse protection of a huge oak tree next to the grave. The service had been brief much to the relief of the gathering whose sadness was dampened even further by the weather.

Connie was filled with grief over the sudden loss of her father. His heart attack took him away so suddenly. It was even a deeper sadness as she realized he was her last connection to family. She lost her mother five years earlier, and the only relatives she knew of were some distant cousins on the East Coast. Until this very moment, Connie had not realized just how alone she felt. She was the only one left to decide what to do with her dad's clock shop as well as her childhood home where her parents had always resided.

Her parents bought the little shop over 35 years ago, naming it *Clockwork Purple*. Why her parents picked that name was still a mystery to her.

Other than the purple walls and hundreds of clocks in the place, there seemed to be no logic to the name. But she had to admit it was rather memorable; certainly more interesting than if it had been named, Tom's Clock Shop.

Walking back to her car, Connie wondered what her dad would want her to do with the place. He had built a solid reputation as the best clock repairman throughout the surrounding counties.

He could fix any watch or clock. On the other hand, she knew nothing about the business. Her career path took her to culinary school in Paris and then to a job as a chef at a popular French restaurant 500 miles away.

Back at her parent's home, Connie greeted friends and neighbors as they came by to give their condolences. She struggled to be appreciative while surrounded by the sea of guilt she felt for not having visited her dad in over a year. The demands of her chef's job had taken all of her time and attention. Lately it had even been difficult to squeeze in a weekly telephone call to her dad.

She was beginning to realize how her dedication to her career had robbed her of a personal life. She hardly noticed how living with constant stress was affecting her. She was tired and lonely. She didn't even have time for a social life, so there was no mate to help share her grief.

The crowd of visitors was dwindling when the

next-door neighbor came by to pay his respects. Connie's dad had told her how kind and helpful the new neighbor had been. He often mentioned how the young man would stop by to chat and play a game of checkers. He even helped repair the porch railing.

"Hi, I'm the next-door neighbor, Ted Watkins," he said as he extended his hand in greeting. "I'm so sorry about your dad. I'm going to miss my visits with him."

"I'm Connie. Thank you for coming by. When I talked to dad a few weeks ago he mentioned how much he enjoyed your visits and willingness to help him from time to time. Thank you for that."

Ted seemed so friendly, and offered to help put some of the food away that people had brought to the house. He was so easy to talk to that Connie not only ended up sharing her concern about what to do with the clock shop, but actually admitted her regret at not having taken the time to visit her dad. She didn't realize how much she needed someone to talk to about something other than what needed to be done at work.

Out of the blue, Ted asked her the most unexpected question, "Have you ever had any dreams other than being a prestigious chef at a fancy restaurant?"

Musing over his question, Connie realized she did have a hidden desire to one day return to her hometown and open a little café. She often longed for a simpler life filled with less stress and more time off.

Without much hesitation, she shared her dream and actually found herself smiling at the thought.

Ted returned her smile, then said, "What would happen if Clockwork Purple turned into your dream café? Clockwork could reflect the history of the place, and purple could represent the royal welcome you would give your patrons. You might even incorporate your dad's clock collection as part of the décor."

Connie was overjoyed at the possibility. As heavy as her heart had been the past few days, she suddenly felt lighter. Turning Clockwork Purple into a café would not only extend her dad's legacy, but also begin a new direction in her life; one with less stress and perhaps with the encouragement of a new friend named, Ted.

A Poem By Dell Blackman

What Is Life

What is life
but, joy
waiting
in the wings
for your call
What is life
but, love
trying to seep
through every crack
in the wall
What is life
but, struggling
to see
that there
is no struggle
at all.

Prompt #2

For Eddie, Music Was More Than Just Sound

AINGEAL ROSE O'GRADY

The sound of the drums seemed especially loud today for Eddie. *I wish they'd stop that racket,* he thought. It wasn't unusual to hear the drummers practicing in the high school marching band. They were often on the football field doing their programs and marches.

For some reason, today the sounds annoyed Eddie. The imperfections and disharmonies wore on him like fingernails on a chalkboard.

For Eddie, music was more than just sound. Music was the very essence of creation, he often thought. He'd give anyone a chance to get the harmony perfect, but after a while he'd lose patience altogether. He found it insulting to distort heaven's frequencies with what he termed, *racket.*

Eddie was five years old when he learned to play his first instrument. At two, he loved listening to music and would often sit with his ear pressed against the Victrola. He loved the sounds of the orchestras and the singing.

Eddie could easily pick out the various instruments, naming them out loud one by one to his nanny. He'd been asking for a flute ever since he was three and now at last he had one. It was a reminder of Home to him.

Now, at 16 he could play many instruments — violin, piano, the sax and horns. He planned on a career in music. It had been what he wanted his entire life thus far.

He couldn't wait for the day to be over. He felt restless and anxious. It wasn't just the drums in the marching band, it was *every* sound. As the day wore on, people's voices seemed louder, footsteps sounded thunderous. Even the faintest sound echoed loudly in his ears. Thinking he was coming down with something, Eddie thought he'd make it through the last two hours of school and get it over with. That was until his ears suddenly fell silent and his vision disappeared. Black silence and black vision were all he was aware of.

Then he hit the ground, falling into unconsciousness. Oddly, Eddie found himself awake in his unconscious state. He heard music — only this time it was the heavenly music he remembered as a child. His environment was a vista of meadows filled with colorful flowers and sweet perfume scents. *Truly I am in Heaven*, he thought, and as fast as that thought came, the next instant he was waking to a bright light being directed toward his eyes by an intern in the ER.

His sight and hearing had both returned and the only remnant of his earlier collapse was a pounding headache. The remainder of the day was spent going through numerous tests designed to uproot the cause of his episode.

After all tests proved to be clear, Eddie was released the following day. He was assigned to bedrest for the rest of the week to which he welcomed, as it gave him time to listen to the three new albums his grandparents had sent him.

On the third day after his release from the hospital, Eddie once again lost his hearing and sight suddenly and from no apparent cause. Like before, he found himself awake in another place, hearing the same familiar music and being surrounded by the brilliance and scents of flowers.

This time, however, he was not a young man but an old man. He was himself for sure, but he had aged by 76 years, or so it seemed. His hair had grayed and his skin had changed, but his hearing and vision were more acute than ever.

Once again, he awoke to find himself in the emergency room being subjected to another battery of uncomfortable tests. In between, he would fall into a vivid dreamstate in which he was traveling back and forth between the world of Heaven and the world of Earth. In each dream, the distance between the two worlds shortened until they were one flowing movement for him.

The second battery of tests showed nothing unusual and like before, Eddie was sent home. What transpired the following days was anybody's guess. Eddie kept it all to himself except to say he was no longer the same person. In fact, he was no longer a person at all in the ways we think of as normal. He had become the bridge between Heaven and Earth. But that's another story!

HARRIETTE HOOVER GREEN

"Oh, isn't he just adorable, Tom? His big brown eyes and little ears. Oh, I love him so much! I can't wait to show him off to all our friends and family. We are so blessed!"

It was winter in Bend, Oregon and just mildly cold. The snow had yet to fall. Goodness, last year was a record breaker. People had to shovel their roofs, or hire it done. Some homes had four feet or more of accumulated snow on their roofs. I heard one of the roofs of a middle school caved in because of the snow. Some people had difficulty with the exhaust pipes on their roof being covered. Well, none of that yet for us. *We are as happy as two bugs in a rug*, thought Susan, as the saying goes.

Eddie was a surprise and was not planned. It was a delightful accident. He was just perfect in every way!

"Let's plan the guest list for his coming- out -party. Shall we invite Mark and Patty, Daryl and Deanna, and oh yes, Elissa and Bob? Too bad Madelyn and Pat moved to New Mexico. Well then, there is Charles and Douglas and Lawrence, and Miranda and Cheryl, Vivian and Richard. Oh my, I think I'm getting carried away! Best we decide on an expense limit and menu before I keep going. I just know everyone will want to come see him!"

Susan quickly ran though her favorite party foods to serve and decided on a non-alcoholic punch, and one Champagne. She was busy making notes while Tom held Eddie and just looked at him as if he was *to the moon*.

"Honey, can you put Eddie down for a minute and help me get these punch bowls down to wash them?" Then she said out loud to herself, "I think I'll run everything through the dishwasher — the bowls, serving bowls and all the glasses and punch cups."

Eddie started wiggling and Tom went back to hold him and he settled immediately.

"Honey, why not rock him and hum a little song. How about, *Oh, Danny Boy*? I've always loved that song. And in place of Danny, just put in Eddie's name. That would be perfect."

Susan was in an especially good mood. She had her boy she'd wanted for such a long time. And now she would get to show him off to everyone. She will be so proud. Plus, Tom was happy with Eddie as well. "We are now a little family."

She called all the people on the guest list after adding Gail and Kevin. However did she forget them? "I must be getting addled in my old age," she thought.

Everyone was able to come but Pat and Mark. "Well, there will be a picture," she told them over the phone.

From there she went into a cleaning frenzy. The house was spotless after three days of intensive work.

"Why do you do that to yourself, Susan?" asked Tom, "Nobody cares if the house is clean!"

"I know, I just feel better when everything is in order," replied Susan.

After the cleaning frenzy she began the cooking marathon. "Oh goodness, the house smells delicious!" After two days of cooking and preparing she felt things were in hand and she could indeed rest for the next two days and just putter and decorate a wee bit. Of course, Eddie was totally unaware of all the fuss his arrival was causing. He was blissfully happy in his little bed.

Suddenly, Susan thought, *Goodness, he doesn't move around very much. He seems happy to just lie there most of the time.*

"Tom, Tom, come here!" Tom was in his den working on a project, but lovingly joined Susan in the day room.

"Tom, have you noticed anything odd about Eddie?"

"What is it?" Tom asked, recognizing the expression of worry on Susan's face.

"Tom, Eddie doesn't move around and just seems content to lie there."

"You're right. I thought it was normal."

"No! That is not normal," said Susan, coming out of her bliss. "Oh my, no, that is not normal; where has my mind been? I've been blind."

Susan picked up Eddie and studied his face. As she looked intently at Eddie she noticed his eyes didn't move. She moved her head from side to side, but Eddie didn't track her movement with his eyes.

"Tom! I don't think Eddie can see. I think he is blind!" Tears popped from her eyes and then a wail and sobs followed. "Our Eddie is blind. Oh, Tom!"

They called the doctor and made an emergency appointment to take Eddie in for a professional assessment. *Maybe there is a way to fix it since he is so young.* At the office the doctor examined Eddie.

"Susan, I think you are right about Eddie. Of course, I will have to do more tests, but he definitely isn't tracking."

They put Eddie on the floor to see what he would do and he just sat there, then lay down. "Here Eddie, here Eddie," Susan called anxiously. Eddie moved toward the sound, wiggled his little body and wagged his tail, and nuzzled her hand.

"Oh sweetheart, I love you so." She swooped him up and snuggled him to her face and let his little baby doggy breath fill her nose. "I've got it! I know what we will do for Eddie," she exclaimed to Tom and the vet.

"We will train him with music. We will put music in his bed for comfort, so that he doesn't feel alone.

That is why he stays still, he can't see. Then we will put the music on a wagon and pull it around to get Eddie moving."

Tom talked with some of his engineering friends about how to make a moving wagon for Eddie to encourage him to follow the sound of music. *For Eddie, music was more than just sound*, it was a tracking device to move him through the house safely. Together Tom and his friends created a battery run wagon with a small battery powered computer that could be programed to run certain routes. It went from his bed to the back door where his food dish was, around the furniture, from the back door down the sidewalk to the trees and the grassy area selected for him to potty. It followed a route to the back door, with an artificial bark to announce he was back, then it went from the back door through the kitchen to his bed. He could live a pretty normal life after all.

Of course, the party was a great success. After all, most retired folk love their pets as much as they love their children. They all oohed and ahhed over Eddie and thought he was the cutest little guy they had ever seen. Stay tuned for more adventures with Eddie!

KEVIN O'GRADY

Eddie moved the slider higher on his new Behringer sound desk. He was sure he heard his dead wife speaking to him from beneath the waves of sound recorded earlier at the National Concert Hall. The Christmas performance of Handel's Messiah had been ecstatic and he found himself transported back in time to its original performance in Dublin on April 13, 1742. The audience then had swelled to over 700 as the ladies had heeded the managements pleas to wear dresses without hoops in order to make room for more company in the great music hall on Fishamble Street near Christchurch Cathedral.

Eddie's wife had been a singer too, and she had invited him to her performance of Handel's Messiah on their first date. She looked ravishing in her hooped gown as there was far more room on the modern stage for the lavishly dressed ladies of the choir.

Eddie got the sound engineers contract for all the shows after that, but this Christmas, it was very different. His wife was dead.

Eddie's hands trembled on the sound desk. Years of recording experience had trained his ear so finely that he could hear a pin drop in an auditorium of thousands. There was no mistaking her voice.

"Eddie," she said softly, "I love you."

Eddie restarted the recording from the beginning, and moved a few more sliders and pressed a few more buttons to enhance the lower frequencies and diminish the higher ones. Just as the soloists alternated with wave upon wave of chorus, and more strongly after the line, "Comfort ye, comfort ye my people, saith your God," he heard it clearly. There was no mistaking it this time.

"Eddie, I love you!"

For Eddie, music was more than just sound, but this experience was defying all his preconceived ideas about life and death.

"It's not possible," Eddie said out loud. Lately he talked to himself more than ever. In some strange way, it seemed to comfort him in her absence. Then, in the middle of the oratorio, on the wave of the crescendoing chorus of the passion of Christ, she whispered back, "Oh, yes it is!"

"Gloria, is that you?" Eddie sat back on the studio chair so the tears rolling down his cheeks would not drip onto the sensitive electronics.

"Yes, Eddie, I'm here."

Eddie raced the recording back to the beginning again. This time he increased the treble and slid the vocals of the chorus to maximum. He repositioned his headphones, pressing them with both hands into his head so he would not hear the distraction from their only daughter playing at the foot of the stairs.

"Gloria, are you there?"

This time he heard the soloist, and then the chorus, building and growing the energy of the famous Hallelujah Chorus to a joyful crescendo. But there was no Gloria. Over and over he listened, but Gloria was gone.

Eddie went to the window. The postman had arrived. He was growing tired of the reminders that continued to arrive in the mail for his famous wife, even though her last performance in the Opera House had occurred almost a Christmas ago.

Sifting through the foreign stamps and the junk mail, he found one in beautiful scripted handwriting. It was addressed to him. Carefully cutting open the envelope with his silver letter opener, he held the letter up to the light and put on his gold-rimmed reading glasses.

In the beautiful handwriting of a patron, the letter began.

I know your precious Gloria is gone, but I always hear her sing to me when I listen to Handel's Messiah. I remember when you first met, and your love for Gloria and Handel's Messiah blossomed at the same time. I swear the oratorio was written for her, because as she sings, she strings my heart along with every symphonic movement through the Nativity, the Passion, the Resurrection, and the Ascension of our Lord Jesus Christ. She sings God's glory in the Hallelujah Chorus like a lark in the clear air, but Eddie, it's the voice that I hear in my head that demands I write to you today.

I swear I hear her speak to me. I hear her say, "Write to Eddie and tell him I love him. And tell him to find a copy of Handel's manuscript."

Eddie ran to his desk and fumbled through the pile of papers he kept of every performance he recorded. On the last page of the dog-eared manuscript was an inscription by Handel himself that read, *SDG—Soli Deo Gloria—to God alone the glory!*

For Eddie, music was more than just sound; it was inspiration. He had no explanation as to how or why it triggered certain feelings and made his heart sing. Since he was born he had been exposed to a variety of music. His parents frequently listened to operas and symphony arrangements of classical music, while his older siblings enjoyed the latest pop songs. Even from a very early age he could pick out and identify the various instruments and the sounds they made. He simply loved music.

In school, he would often be caught daydreaming; his attention span was below par. Yet when he studied while listening to music, he was often so inspired that the work he did was well beyond his own understanding.

Realizing he had a tough time in school when other kids teased him and teachers often criticized him for his lack of attention, his parents surprised him with a guitar when he was ten years old. They hoped to give him a musical outlet for his love of music.

Much to the disappointment of his parents, the guitar sat in its case. Eddie could not make music with the strings; he preferred listening to it.

Eddie was bullied at school because he was not into sports and other typical school activities. He would stick to himself listening to music for hours. There was hardly a time he didn't have ear buds stuck in his ears.

In his senior year of high school, a new music teacher took a personal interest in this young man who loved music so much, but didn't play an instrument. The teacher discovered that Eddie could not only read music, he also had an exceptional talent for composing original creations. Realizing this, the music teacher invited Eddie to lead the school band in his own arrangement of their school's fight song for the next school rally.

Eddie was challenged by the opportunity and created the most uplifting and inspiring version anyone had ever heard. As he conducted the school's band and experienced the positive reaction of the student body, he realized he could create magic with music. For the first time in his life he understood how to tap into people's emotions and lift their spirits.

The music teacher had opened a door for Eddie that took him on an inspired journey to become one of the world's most renowned musical conductors in the country. For Eddie, music was more than just sound; it was his inspired life.

Lending The Gift

Before ...
the day has closed,
listen with your heart
and wrap kindness
around the shoulders
of a troubled soul
Let judgement ...
find someone else
to control
Stay free and clear
of the appetite
that feeds
a gossiping mind
Noble is a nod
to the heavens
when lending the gift
of being kind.

Prompt #3

He Took A Few Steps
As If Walking Upright

AINGEAL ROSE O'GRADY

Jacob stood at the cathedral entrance and took in its magnificence. He had never seen such an awe inspiring display of religious icons, flying buttresses and gargoyles. He wondered about the gargoyles — such distorted faces and for what purpose? He had heard it was to ward off evil spirits, but why need them when the cathedral was supposed to be a holy place filled with angels and the spirits of saints.

Jacob slowly made his way to the cathedral entrance, noticing the smells of lilacs coming from the row of trees alongside the entrance to the right. They were purple and white and their fragrance set the stage for entering this holy place.

The large arched wooden doors were already opened. Tourists from around the world were making their way into this famous place filled with history and legends. It wasn't just the magnificence of the architecture, it was the stories that had been told down through the ages that brought visitors to this place.

There were relics in this cathedral. The veil of the Virgin Mary was said to be framed beside an altar dedicated to her and pieces of the original cross of Jesus were encased in a golden box with a glass lid near another altar.

But it was what was in the basement of this cathedral that had held the most mystery. It was rumored that an old crypt was held beneath the layers of limestone in the cathedral — the occupant unknown. Some said it was the remains of St. Peter while others said it was one of the Knights Templar. And still others went so far as to say it was the remains of Mary Magdalene. The crypt had never been opened, adding to its mystery.

But none of this was what interested Jacob. His gaze kept turning upwards towards the ceiling of the cathedral. The decorated arches were vast and expansive and each told a different biblical story. It was designed to send the viewers into ancient times when Jesus lived and ultimately received his ascension. It was meant to arouse emotional feelings of devotion and it did its job well.

Jacob found his curiosity being piqued as he noticed a small curved stairway behind the main altar at the back of the cathedral. It was hardly noticeable in the dim light, as if it was meant to be concealed from the public eye. But some strange force was driving Jacob closer and closer to the stairway. He knelt down on the kneelers that ran in an arced flow in front of the main altar along with other tourists to appear as normal as possible.

His heart was pounding with anticipation as to where the stairway led. *How am I going to get closer*, he thought, *with so many tourists here?* There was no break in the endless stream of them filling the large attraction. He decided he would just behave as if he worked there and belonged there. He held his woolen cap in his hands respectfully and rose from the kneelers, making a small sign of the cross. *He took a few steps as if walking upright* and proceeded to make his way past the red lit candles placed in front of the statue of Mary. He opened the small side gate that led to the area behind the main altar. No one seemed to think anything of it — it was assumed he had permission.

Jacob walked quickly past the main altar until he was behind it and out of sight. The curved stairway was narrow and long, but he placed his foot upon it anyway and began his ascent, taking care to be soundless as he went.

A flock of birds suddenly panicked and flew away when they sensed his approach. Jacob felt a cold breeze envelope him as he neared the top. When he arrived, he was met by a small wooden door that was strangely designed with more gargoyle faces arranged in geometric patterns on the doors midsection. They gave the appearance of a warning and Jacob stopped to contemplate his next move.

I have been guided here, he thought. *I should follow this through.*

He stepped forward slowly, intending to turn the old brass doorknob. But again he stopped. The warning energy was palpable, even menacing. Once again, he re-examined his motives. Yes, he had been guided here. He would do it! As his right-hand fell on the doorknob, a rush of light penetrated through the keyhole. Surprisingly, the door was unlocked. Jacob opened the door and stepped inside. A large coffin was set in the center of the small round room. Upon it was a Latin inscription.

In Filiis Hominum Peccatte (the sins of mankind).

Jacob froze in his tracks. He knew then that his life was over.

HARRIETTE HOOVER GREEN

Winston seemed slower than normal—his balance had been off and he often walked at a tilt. Vivian was worried, but he just poo-pooed it. "I'm fine, I'm just working too hard and sitting too long which makes my lower half get a bit numb." "Oh honey, numb?" Vivian asked. "No, not really numb, sort of like a charley-horse, you know what I mean. I'm fine," Winston responded.

Winston, named after Sir Winston Churchill, was a hard driving Senator from Oregon. His father was an attorney who ran for the Mayor's office and won. Winston grew up in the limelight of fame, even though it was a small town and it was small fame. He was liked by everyone from the time he was a boy to this very day. He loved his work and his constituents loved him, the good Democrat that he was. He had followed politics from his early teen years, having long talks with his dad, watching CNN and Charlie Rose on television.

He worked so hard because he cared so much about his state and the people he represented, even those from the other party. However, he didn't do good self care, he didn't exercise and he didn't eat right. He quit smoking several times, then he would go back to it like an old friend you would call when you needed to ponder something. And recently, he needed to ponder this issue of the water use and Mirror Pond. The people felt strongly about the water, the land use, the parks and trails and the tourists, especially in Bend, Oregon where he grew up. Living in Eugene seemed like a foreign place, but Bend was too remote from the legislature. He needed to fly out often to other cities in the state and off to Washington, D.C.

"Vivian, do you know where I put my glasses, I've looked everywhere." "Winston, they are on your head!" They laughed simultaneously; they loved each other and had been together so long they were almost like one unit with two bodies. "Let me make you a cup of tea", Vivian suggested. "What kind would you like?"

"I'd rather have a scotch," Winston replied. "Winston, please let's wait till this evening and I'll make you a nice scotch, but now a cup of tea is in order." She went to the kitchen and sorted through their tea supply looking for something he might like that would give him a boost. She settled on licorice and made him a strong cuppa, as her mom used to say. As she was bringing him the tea she heard a crash.

"Winston! Winston!" When she reached him he was down on the carpet, having crashed into a table and knocking the lamp off, but the table cushioned the fall. "Winston, Winston, can you hear me?" His eyes were open, he seemed to be conscious, but he was not responding to her voice.

She took his hand and squeezed it, no response. She rushed to the phone and called 911, asking for an ambulance. "I think my husband has had a stroke, hurry!" She ran to the bathroom to the medicine cabinet looking for the aspirin. She grabbed the bottle, opening it as she ran back to the study. The tea was in the kitchen — it would be too hot. She rushed back to Winston. He was still in a daze. His eyes did not track her. She put the aspirin under his tongue, knowing it would dissolve, not wanting him to choke on water. It was a very small thing to do to avoid blood clotting. It was all she could do for now.

She sat on the floor trying to make him as comfortable as she could, cradling his head in her lap and covering him with a blanket. He was a big man, six foot tall and over 230 pounds. *Where is that ambulance*, she thought? Hurry, hurry! She stroked his beautiful white, wavy hair, not like Reagan's, more like Kennedy's hair, but white. She talked to him in soothing, calm tones assuring him he would be fine. "Winston, you're a tough old bird, we will laugh about this ungraceful tumble!" By now Winston's eyes were closed, which worried her greatly.

"Winston, I'm here, I'm here." She heard the siren's wail getting closer. "Dear God, thank you!"

The rescue squad found their way in through the front door. She called out, "Go straight and turn right, we are in the study!" They had the gurney and two of them lifted Winston onto the portable bed. They rolled up a towel and put it under his head to assure he did not choke on his own saliva, as many people do who have had strokes.

As she looked at him on the gurney, she could see that one side of his face was slacked. His color was grey and he was mumbling something and gurgling his saliva.

"Winston, swallow, swallow!" yelled Vivian. He began choking on his own saliva. "Do something!", she yelled at the three guys in white. One of the guys jumped into action, grabbed Winston sitting him up and forcing his head forward. Winston swallowed, "Thank God!" she said aloud.

She followed the ambulance to the hospital. When they exited the house, all the neighbors were lining the sidewalk with very worried expressions on their faces. "Oh, Vivian, what do you need, how can I help?" asked her good friend and neighbor, Avis.

"Could you drive me to the hospital, my hands are shaking so bad I don't think I can drive."

"Of course," said Avis as she rushed to get her car. "I'll stay with you. You need someone with you."

At the hospital the doctor in the ER confirmed

that Winston had a stroke. They would not know the extent of the damage until the results of the MRI and his blood work returned, but at least he was alive. Once settled in his room, she soothed him, stroking his hair and talking softly to him, assuring him it would be all right, that he would be all right.

She sat with him through the night, sending her neighbor home. "I can take a taxi if I decide to go home. Please go home Avis, please." As she sat through the night, Winston remained in a sort of coma with his eyes closed. She talked to him constantly assuring him she was there, that he would be all right, and that she was all right.

She went on to say, "Maybe now we can take that trip around the world we promised to take one day. Winston, you must stop driving yourself. You must really address your health!" Talking was the only way she could push the fear away and prevent her mind from going to, *what if.*

He was up and having a liquid breakfast when she entered the room a week later. "Today's the day!," he said. "They are going to get me up and see how well I can walk." Once up, *he took a few steps as if walking upright,* but his body was at a tilt. It would be a long way back. He realized there is more to life than work!

KEVIN O'GRADY

Rob McRae's death notice appeared in all the usual newspapers. For such a famous Scotsman, his passing seemed dramatic, yet for him it was seamless. It was like *he took a few steps as if walking upright* for the first time in his life, but he wasn't alive.

Rob could see the ambulance crew around his body, all resigned to the fact that they had lost him. The wreckage of his car lay off to the roadside, and the driver of the truck that had hit him sat in the back seat of the flashing police car with his face in his hands. Rob was aware of everything, every spoken word, even every thought that everyone around was thinking.

How is this possible? Surely my mind would be overwhelmed by the amount of data and detail.

But Robert McRae's mind was no ordinary mind. His extensive studies into the phenomena of time-travel and near-death-experience had expanded his mind to accepting a new world of all possibilities, one not limited by the confines, limitations, or restrictions of his earthly body. It was this exploring mindset, this expansion of consciousness that had drawn the attention of the futurists like a moth to a candle flame.

His fame spread far and wide as one who could not only empathize with near death experiencers, but he could enter into their experience with them. He could see and feel what they saw and felt, but what's more, he could stay in the experience at will and explore those places beyond the veil of human understanding for as long as he wanted. It was then he discovered that he could alter the future.

"He did this on purpose," he could hear the truck driver say. "He did this to prove something. He did this so he could experience it himself. He caused the accident himself. He forced me to crash into him."

"Wait, what?" The policeman had turned around from the driver seat, notebook in hand to question the truck driver. "Are you sure? How do you know that?"

Rob McRae watched the logic of the human brain analyze the situation. He fascinated at the huge assumptions the mind made to fill gaps in understanding. He marveled at the incessant human need to apportion blame, to divide, to separate, and to decide guilt or innocence.

He watched the accident scene quickly develop into a crime scene, while all the time he was removed from the anxiety of it all. He was not a part of the panic. He had no sense of dread, or loss, or pain, or suffering.

On the contrary, his comprehension was so huge that he could understand for the first time how creative humanity really is. He could connect the dots between cause and effect without the interference of time. But most amazing of all was his ability to change the outcome of the future.

They're going to arrest that truck driver. They will try to charge him with murder.

Rob McRae's vision went back in time to just before the accident. He watched the progression develop before his eyes. He watched as the electrons shifted and coalesced like pixels in a Disney movie. He heard the thoughts of the truck driver just before the accident.

That's Rob McRae. He thinks he can change the future. I'll show him.

Suddenly, the truck driver changed lanes, lurching the huge truck across the median line in an attempt to mangle Rob into the guardrails. Rob and his brand-new Audi were about to be crushed like biscuit crumbs. As Rob watched the inevitability of the accident unfold before his eyes, the phone rang beside the truck driver.

"Hi, this is Dr. Rob McRae's office. I'm calling to confirm your appointment today with Dr. McRae." The ringing of the phone shocked the driver back into the realization of what he was about to do. Within inches of mangling the Audi, he lurched the huge rig back into his own lane, pulling the chain of his air horn in answer to the cacophony of blowing horns from the drivers witnessing the near accident.

Rob McRae zoomed back in time to when the truck driver first came into his office. He watched his new patient lie back on the leather couch and adjust himself nervously.

"I've had a vision of the future," the truck driver said. "I killed you with my truck on Highway 101."

"Okay, let's relax," Rob said calmly. He took a few steps back from the couch and pressed the secretary's button on the intercom. "Freda, no calls. We are going into a future-altering session right away. And please cancel my death notice out of the morning newspaper."

He took a few steps as if walking upright for the first time. There were flashing lights all around him. Where were they coming from? He heard muffled voices that sounded as if they were speaking in some foreign tongue. Where was he and why were there so many strange-looking forms swarming around him? Kirby's body felt so heavy, as if he had just broken free from a pool of thick, wet cement. He tried to keep walking, but his legs refused to move. He was fading in and out of consciousness.

He was being propelled in some way, but he couldn't be sure just how. There was something or someone on each side of him. There were other silhouettes moving around, but they seemed more interested in the wreckage he had just fled, than his well-being. Flames were shooting up from the debris. His eyes refused to stay open.

The heat from the flames was growing hotter, and Kirby knew instinctively that it was a good thing he was being moved away from the blaze.

Suddenly, there was a loud explosion and he felt himself moving even faster away from the sound. How could this be? He could not feel himself moving any body parts, yet he had the sensation of being propelled quickly through the darkness. Then he caught a brief glimpse of a dark form next to him. Maybe he was being carried. At that he blacked out.

"Sir, sir," pleaded a voice above him. "Please open your eyes!"

Kirby tried to do as requested, however his eyelids would not respond. Thoughts were swimming through his head.

Where am I? What has happened? Who are these people?

He tried to utter words, but could not even make a sound with his voice. And, once again he faded out of reality, as if locked in a deep, dark cave.

At some point, Kirby became vaguely aware of the voices around him, even though he was unable to understand much of what he heard. Then his eyes opened for just a second or two before they closed from the heaviness of his eyelids.

What had he caught a glimpse of? There were several dark shapes against what looked like a night sky with clouds blacking out the stars.

It was so dark, so strange. And, he noticed flashing lights behind the forms. They didn't look human, which confused Kirby. Was he in some strange part of the world? Why couldn't he remember? In and out of consciousness, there were moments of clarity.

At one point, Kirby realized he was laying on the ground, covered with some kind of warm covering. He couldn't move any part of his body, and the only pain he had was a terrible headache. He felt like an alien from another planet. Nothing seemed real; nothing made sense.

Someone was trying to get him to wake up. He had a sensation of movement as if his whole body was being pushed or nudged. Slowly his eyes opened and he was staring into the eyes of someone bending over him. He strained to gain visual clarity. There was no sensation of the time of day or no way of knowing how long he had been lying on the ground. Kirby had no voice to ask for answers, or to even tell this man that he couldn't feel his arms or legs.

"You've been in a plane crash, sir," said the man. "You are going to be okay, however we have to get you to a hospital right away."

Kirby was more confused than ever. A plane crash? He didn't even remember being on an airplane. Where would he have been going? With his vision restored, Kirby could see that the man talking to him was wearing a black coat and a brimmed hat. His shape blended into the dark sky, while the flashing lights added an eerie glow behind him. The scene was something out of a movie.

Suddenly, he heard childlike voices, "Daddy, daddy, wake up. It's time to take us to baseball practice!"

Kirby struggled to open his sleepy eyes. *Could it be*, he wondered? Through his grogginess, he could see the eager faces of his two sons. What a great way to wake up!

A POEM BY DELL BLACKMAN

Off The Shelf

As I start to wake up
Still lying in my bed
I see all these images
Floating inside my head
Fragments of the daydream
I'm slowly entering into
Some I give attention
For a quick review
Rehearsing my role
I refresh my other self
Like putting on clothes
I've taken off the shelf.

Prompt #4

I Burned My Hand Badly
While Holding A Red
And Green
Fire Cone

I stood gazing out the window at the drops of fresh spring rain as they landed on the long balsam needles belonging to the old fir tree in my backyard. The sound of the drops as they slowly rolled down the needles and landed on the dark brown earth below put me in an altered state as I sipped my tea. I don't know how long I stood there — I had drifted off into another time in my life and another place. I was remembering when *I burned my hand badly while holding a red and green fire cone.*

It was on the camping trip with David, my former lover. It was our last camping trip together. We had been arguing again about my children and we were both tired of it. He was setting up the tent and I was arranging the sticks for the campfire. I had put two fire cones amongst the kindling and had lit a match to get it started.

We continued to argue about the time spent with

my children. David had no children of his own and I considered his lack of experience the basis of his inability to understand parenthood.

At one point in the conversation I was reacting violently to something he said while adjusting the sticks in the fire. I was not paying attention and I had picked up one of the fire cones without looking and the rest is history. You could say that the burn matched the intensity of my mood at the time, although the aftereffects are still felt today.

The scarring from that experience both physically and emotionally still inhibits my flexibility in matters relating to change and commitment. My relationship with David ended after that weekend and it came as no surprise to either of us. I could not concede to spending less time with my children and he could not adapt to the family unit that had already been created by my former marriage.

Although my relationship with David has ended six months ago, I still find myself drifting back to our time together, rehashing memories and conversations as if they had just occurred. I have become reclusive since then, preferring to stay inside by the fire blanketed by the softly knit afghan my mother sent to me the year before her passing. I wished she was here now so I could rest my tired soul in her bosom. Mom had always been such a source of comfort and consolation for me and now I am left to tend to my wounds on my own.

I heard through the grapevine that David has already moved on. He is living with a new love; a young professional woman with no children. I wondered about that — how people move on so quickly from one another.

Was there no remorse, no sorrow about lost love these days? Does the heart not need tending to in these post relationship moments?

Here am I, still mourning over my lost love, and there is he, happily sharing himself with another. It left me feeling numb.

Shaking myself out of my reverie, I forced myself to do something different with this day. I got dressed and packed my camera in the car along with a picnic basket and a bottle of wine. I would drive until I found a spot that inspired me, if there was such a place these days.

The clock in my car now said 1 p.m. and I suddenly turned to the left down a long and winding road. The road was smooth and the sloping terrain opened to a vast vista of wildflowers and berries.

I got out of my car and began snapping photos of the beauty and openness all around me. My camera honed in on butterflies dancing from flower to flower, stamens and petals with intricate designs, blades of grass in yellows and greens and blue skies with patches of clouds.

It was a simple scene really, but for some reason, I found myself becoming uplifted and filled with joy.

This simple open place had opened my mind and shone some light in. I decided right then and there that moments like these would be my new passion and my new search. I would spend my time looking for the mystical and the inspiring and then freeze frame those places with my camera. Driving home, I felt peace enter me for the first time in months. I had finally come out of the darkness.

CHARLES SCAMAHORN

Where to begin telling the problems that erupted that dark and stormy night? We had ascended a cliff on Mt. Boring to near a small flat area we had spotted from below and where we intended to set up our overnight camp. It was a perfect day for climbing and camping when we left our cars at a wide place in the dirt road a couple of miles below, but the trail became more difficult than expected and we had wasted an hour on a wrong turn on a confusing fork in the trail.

We chose the trail less used but it appeared to be pointed up the direction we were intending to go. It ended up an hour later at a large hole in the ground where some crazy miner probably thought there was something worth digging for and he wasted a month. We only wasted an hour on that detour, but it was an hour that later became critical and brought on our crisis. Let me mention at this point that if you find this bottle, I survived. At least I survived hanging off the cliff long enough to write this essay.

You see, we were stuck right here all night while lightning intermittently exposed our perilous situation, and pounding wind peeled my friends off the cliff and into the oblivion below. At least while I write this it looks like oblivion. I can see nothing but swirling fog. Perhaps if you find this on a perfectly clear day, like the one we were having such a wonderful time enjoying only a few hours ago, you will see how beautiful Mother Nature can be.

However, if you notice piles of human remains below you might get a deeper appreciation of how dangerous our universal mother can be and how her beauty can suddenly turn into your personal ugliness and horror.

I am functionally tied to this crack in the cliff face by my improvised support made of the shoulder straps of my pack wrapped around my thermos bottle and jammed into the crack. I hang here! I'm filled with guilt for leading my friends into this absurd situation and hearing them curse me as they fell from the cliff below — one by one. But what could I do? What can I do now?

In a last desperate effort to summon help, while my remaining friends were clinging to the cliff face below, I wiggled out the rescue flare. It was a flare to be used when lost and a rescue party or search airplane was overhead, but here in the wind and fog, it was useless. All the same, they called from below in their desperation for me to do something! Anything!

With an impossible twisting about while hanging there in my improvised straitjacket that Houdini would have respected, I succeeded in lighting the flare.

I burned my hand badly while holding a red and green fire cone. I was waving it wildly and screaming at the top of my already raw voice. There wasn't any reasonable hope of a savior even hearing me, or any of us; we had all screamed our life out into the fog from a mountain named *Boring* in the middle of a place on our map named *Nowhere*.

Harriette Hoover Green

I stretched and yawned and opened my eyes to a brilliant sunshiny day, and sighed a sigh of joy! Beautiful, exquisite, perfect! As I smiled, I arose and wrapped my silk robe around my tall, trim body and walked over to the window to see the sea. Beautiful, exquisite, perfect, alive!

I felt like I was in a sort of heaven, everything was perfect. I felt buoyant, as though floating on air as I moved around my spacious, beautifully decorated room, large enough to be an apartment. I went to the lavatory to splash my face, clean my mouth and comb my hair before settling into my meditation chair.

I was eager to go inside to learn what would surface from my subconscious mind after such a lovely, deep, refreshing sleep. Initially, in the meditation there was only dark, empty space with no thoughts, no emotions and no feelings. Then my memory brought forth the party on the Fourth of July. I shifted my thoughts to a blank screen and waited.

This day was too wonderful to reflect on such stupidity.

Back to my meditation. Still there was darkness. I felt a bit restless, nothing was coming. I sat there for the entire 20-minutes dedicated for my morning meditation. *Hmm, that was non-productive, or was it?*

I contemplated that being unable to go into the meditative state suggested I was blocking something. I knew I didn't want to explore what caused me to become so tuned into another that I ignored my own physical feeling of burning.

No time for this now.

I reached for my glass of water and noticed the scar on the back of my hand. I first thought, *Oh how ugly*, then immediately thought how grateful I was, as I had trained my mind to live in love. It was only my hand, which I still had full use of without pain.

The telephone interrupted my thoughts about my hand and I shifted into the present and the list of things I planned to do today. I picked up my computer and checked my calendar for my days appointments.

Hmm, 10:00 a.m. appointment with Mrs. Jean Woolworth, 11:00 a.m. with Mr. Charles LeRoy, 1:00 p.m. appointment with Miss Celeste Strangelove, a 3:00 p.m. with Mr. and Mrs. Joseph Murray, and a 5:00 p.m. appointment with the entire Jones family of eight, parents and children. I had a full day of work!

I wondered what I should wear today that would show I am an excellent therapist.

I want to exude competence and compassion. I want to relate to both men and women, as well as children. Ah, my blue dress with the funky jewelry that children always find fun. What shall I have the children do while the adults sort out what they want help with? Yes, I'll work in the dollhouse room and allow them some time before I enter to observe the dollhouses and dolls. We shall all play dollhouse.

After a brief breakfast of vegetables, one egg and one cup of coffee, I set myself up for my first appointment with Mrs. Woolworth, a very smart and sassy widow who was struggling with the loss of her husband, and the transitions she is now facing. Her life suddenly had turned upside down. At the last appointment she was struggling with her identity, asking, "Who am I now that he is dead? Am I the Bank President's widow, or just Mr. Woolworth's widow? People already treat me differently. It feels like I've lost the status of being the wife of a Bank President to just being a wife! Who am I?"

Where are the notes I made during our last session? I wondered. *I'll have Mrs. Woolworth do some writing about her dilemma using her non-dominant hand. That should reveal her inner voice.*

I looked at my watch for the time as I reached for a drink of water, again noticing the scar on the back of my right hand. I involuntarily reached to touch my right hand with my left and gently touched the scar. I had an immediate flashback to the fire and the pain. I heard the laughter and the music and then the scream coming out of my mouth. Again, I shut down those thoughts and returned to my day's agenda.

Mrs. Woolworth arrived looking angry and lost, but very determined to find her way through the maze of grief. The session went as expected — she raged, then cried and then relaxed into the assignment to write her thoughts with her non-dominant hand. The writings revealed she wanted to make a life for herself as herself, without one of being someone's wife. She teared as she shared that she wanted to go back to school and get a degree. "Yes, I want to be my own person!"

Mr. LeRoy arrived on time, as always. He looked totally in charge and beautifully put together, everything matching perfectly. He spoke in his clipped and organized manner relating his week. He reported he had decided he wanted to take a trip and get away from everything and everyone that was familiar. He wanted to break out of the routine and experience life differently. He was going camping for the first time in his life! *Wow, that was a major change*, I thought. I could not imagine Mr. LeRoy in camping clothes, cooking over a fire. I asked what motivated such a drastic idea. Mr. LeRoy said, "You did! Your story about your burn!"

"My story about my burn?" I asked.

"I am so impressed with how you overcame the embarrassment of burning your own hand by being too involved in listening to another's story. You forgot you were holding the green and red fire cone, until your hand was burning. And then, you minimized the accident and simply put your hand in cold water, then wrapped it with ice packs and went on with the Fourth of July party. You maintained your composure even in pain. You ignored your own needs to address your agenda to be the consummate hostess. And, you were."

Consummate hostess, consummate hostess, oh that does sound a bit smug, I thought. *There it is. That is what I have been pushing down. I'm like Mr. LeRoy (perfect)!* I wanted to scream, *I am anything but perfect, if only you knew. I am covering my imperfections with that facade.*

He said, "I want to break out of that mold of perfection and get loose, be in the moment, not in the image of what I think I am supposed to be or do. You have taught me to live in the now, in the present; you are a great teacher. Thank you. I will call when I return and we will see where to go from here."

Before I could answer, the telephone rang. Ms. Strangelove needed to reschedule, allowing me some time to reflect on Mr. LeRoy's comments. I agreed with his assessment of my reaction to my injury and his assessment of my personality traits that were parallel to his own.

Wonderful, wonderful learning from my patients, wonderful being human, wonderful making mistakes in order to grow. Why else was I in this field, doing this work with humans trying to better themselves?

At that moment I remembered how *I burned my hand badly while holding a red and green fire cone,* and why! I was reflecting on my tendency to present myself as perfect, knowing full well being imperfect would be more helpful to my clients who see themselves as less than everyone else.

I took in a deep breath of gratitude, exhaling the love I felt in my heart for myself and for all living things in existence! Another deep breath inhaling the pain of the Universe and another exhale of love for the Universe and all life inside it, as I transmuted the pain into love. My next appointment and the one's following were more wonderful excursions into the frailties of being human, living on this Earth after coming from the stars.

Kevin O'Grady

Amelia moaned about the pain again, but she was complaining to herself. She was lucky she was not dead. Her hand was raw and inflamed, but she continued to turn the wrench to reattach the radio aerial back onto the old biplane. Her navigation was not in error, it was the yaw from the crosswind that caught her off-guard.

After some moments of sideways drift, she found herself suddenly without upward lift. The air currents in the mountains suddenly changed and her old plane was in a down-draft. Clipping the tops of the trees, she braced herself for the impact. But like trees swaying in a high wind, the trees absorbed most of her plane's impact before eventually coming to rest in a clearing.

She emerged from the plane alive but shocked and with only minor injuries to her hand from the blowback of an exhaust flame through the cockpit.

Nothing caught fire, and nothing was too badly damaged that she couldn't repair herself, but first she must make radio contact.

"This is AE 555 to Dijabi Base. Do you read me? Over!"

She repeated the call over and over but there was no response. As she lay in the heat of the jungle, she felt her courage diminish quickly as the evening drew close. She could hear the sounds of animals and birds, some raucous and loud, others sinister and secretive as they emerged to hunt in the quickly darkening denseness of the forest.

At times, she was sure she could hear deep breathing, and every click in the undergrowth, every broken branch or shuffle from trees had her on edge. Her eyes adjusted to the dimming light as she rushed to create some semblance of a sleeping quarters for herself beside the plane. Without blankets or cushions to sleep on, she quickly made up a makeshift bed from an old tarpaulin and some dried coconut palms. Now she must rest, and continue her repairs to the radio in the morning.

The darkness descended upon her like a heavy blanket, but in place of the nighttime silence that she loved in her native village back home, her ears were near to bursting with the sounds of the activity of the jungle.

In her mind's eye she returned to her childhood where her father was reading her a bedtime story. He had tucked her up in the comfort of her favorite blanket, and to the light of the kitchen peeping through the half-open door, he began to read.

"Amelia rested against the left wing of the plane." His voice was soft and reassuring. Amelia knew he always transposed her name into every story. She loved the way he always brought every story to vivid life by making her the heroine. *"Amelia felt the softness of sleep overcome her,"* he continued.

She knew this was a parent's technique to get their children to sleep, but it wasn't working this time. "Tell me what happened, Dad, what happened?"

"Amelia drifted into the deepest sleep she ever had, and in her dreams she saw an angel come from the sky to rescue her."

"What was she like, Dad?" Amelia asked.

"The angel's name was Erica, and she came and lay down beside Amelia, sheltering her and keeping her warm and safe under the spread of her big wide wings."

Oh, how I wish an angel would come to me now, Amelia thought. *If ever I needed a miracle, it is now!*

Suddenly, the radio crackled into life. "This is Dijabi Base to AE 555. Amelia, do you read me, over?" Amelia raced to the cockpit and in the darkness found and squeezed the transmitter.

"Dad, is that you?"

"Yes, my love. I have triangulated your position. Do you have any injuries? Are you safe to go through the night?" Even through all his anxious questioning his voice was reassuring, and there was a fatherly love and concern about it that made her feel much loved.

"I'm okay," she replied confidently. She knew she must reassure him just as much as she needed his reassurance. "I tried lighting a fire but *I burned my hand badly while holding a red and green fire cone*, but aside from that I'm okay."

"Thank God for that. We have a fix on your position and will be there at first light. I will leave this channel open and I will be here all night if you need to call me."

Amelia was sure she felt the softness of white angel feathers under and over her when she awoke. It was early and the bright light was already streaming through the trees into her bedroom. She must be in school by eight, but oh how her body ached, and the pain from the burn on her hand was intense.

I just know my Dad will give me the day off! she thought, as she turned over on her white feather bed and sank into the softness of her new feather pillow.

Edward stood at the big picture window, frozen in thought and fixated on the valley below. He could think of nothing but the sudden loss of his family, his business, and now his mountain-top home.

Anyone observing the scene would totally misunderstand what had happened to this man of forty something. His statuesque frame and polished appearance did not reflect his burden of grief. He looked like the epitome of success. A few weeks earlier, that would have been a fair assessment, however, that was no longer the case.

"Ed," called a male voice from upstairs, "are you ready to go?" Edward did not bother to answer. He was lost in thought and mourning the recent sequence of events that had changed his life so drastically.

His younger brother, Ryan, called to him again, "Edward, you down there?"

The lack of response brought Ryan hurrying down the stairs. "There you are. Are you ready to go?"

Ryan softened his tone of voice as he reached up to gently pat Edward's shoulder. "It's time."

In silence Edward followed Ryan out the front door, closing it for the last time. Without a word, he slid into the passenger seat of his brother's pickup. The bed of the truck was filled with all the possessions Edward had in the world; all crammed into dozens of cardboard boxes.

The two rode in silence for miles until Ryan couldn't stand the quiet any longer.

"Look, Ed, you have got to pull yourself together somehow. I know you've been through a difficult time, but Carole would hate to see you like this. She loved you so much. Nothing anyone can say will bring her or the baby back. It was a terrible car accident. Who would have known you would be dealt such a terrible hand after just filing bankruptcy the week before. I can not even pretend to know how you feel or even begin to put myself in your shoes, but I do know there has to be a light of hope somewhere. I am so sorry for the pain you are going through. If I could make things better, I would in a heartbeat."

Edward stared straight ahead. Words were locked deep in his throat.

"Hey, it's going to be okay, Ed. I'm here for you, just like you were there for me when *I burned my hand badly while holding a red and green fire cone*. I was only eight years old, but I remember it as if it was yesterday. You got help for me and told me over and over that it was going to be okay. You even offered to do my chores. Remember? I want to be there for you now, like you were for me."

Slowly Edward turned his head to look at Ryan. All he could do was offer a slightly affirmative nod before silently returning his gaze out the windshield.

"We'll get through this together," offered Ryan. "People don't call us the Strong brothers for nothing!"

With that, Edward started to smile ever so slightly at the ridiculousness of his little brother's comment. Breaking his silence for the first time in hours, with a touch of sarcasm Edward said, "They only call us that because Strong is our last name, you twit!"

A POEM BY DELL BLACKMAN

Allowing The Wind

I may not avoid
lightening strikes
I may not see
the signs in the sky
I may not sense a storm
brewing overhead
Nor, understand
the reason why
But, I can respond
with a sailors delight
to every challenge
at sea
I can adjust my sails,
tighten the tethers,
and allow the wind
to carry me.

Prompt #5

I Couldn't Concentrate.
My Thoughts Finned Off
Into The Gloom.

AINGEAL ROSE O'GRADY

It was a desperate attempt really. So dramatic and full of self-serving ego. But I suppose if you're going to leap from the roof of a 50-story building, it could be considered dramatic. How Mr. Globs lived through that ordeal was a mystery to us all. He was, after all, a slight man, 6'3" with deep green eyes and an aging temperament.

He was the storyteller in our apartment building. Every Saturday morning a conglomerate of 15 to 20 children would gather in the lobby eagerly awaiting Mr. Globs' next story. All his stories were fantastic, made up entirely from his own imagination with some personal experiences thrown in. You could witness some adults hiding behind support pillars waiting to hear what would come next.

My favorite was the one about Sharie, a creature that was half mermaid and half fairy. She hadn't quite made the entire transition between the sea and the air, dabbling in both worlds. Hers was a story of identity crisis.

Belonging to two worlds wasn't always easy, especially when you wanted to stay in one world longer than the other but needed to dip in and out of both for survival purposes.

Mr. Globs hadn't mentioned Sharie in over a year so it caught us all off guard when he announced that Saturday's story would be the continued saga of Sharie, the Mermaid Fairy.

Only this time he hung his head low as he began. Sharie, the Mermaid Fairy, had been captured! He had just heard the news. Her fate was unknown. There had only been rumors about who had taken her and why. No further details were given about where she might be — just some speculations.

Upon hearing the news, *I couldn't concentrate, my thoughts finned off into the gloom.*

Why I reacted in such a way surprised even me. It was just a story after all — wasn't it? The children too were tangibly upset with sighs and "Oh's!" and then dead silence. Everyone moved up closer to Mr. Globs, anxiously awaiting what he would say next.

Mr. Globs announced that he knew of only one way to find Sharie. He would have to look for the portal that would take him into the netherworld. The problem was whether it was through the air or the sea.

He asked the children to take a vote — it would be up to them to decide where the portal was. He divided the children up into three groups and gave them 10 minutes to decide and tally up the results.

The children decided the portal had to be through the air since Sharie was last seen out of the sea. They also said that the portal could only be accessed from the top of their apartment building, aptly called the Belle Aire.

Mr. Globs knew what he must do. He would have to gauge the spot on the roof and take a dive into it, trusting he wouldn't end up flat as a pancake on the street below.

It was a risky business, to say the least! Insane really, once we all realized he actually meant to do it! Mr. Globs was turning out to be egocentric — a man wanting to leave this world as a famous risk taker, someone who would be on the nightly news for at least a week or so.

The event was to take place on the following Monday as there was no time to lose. Sharie's life depended on it. This is why it was so amazing that when Mr. Globs leaped from the southeast corner of the roof of the Belle Aire Apartments, he disappeared!

Firemen and paramedics as well as the huge crowd that had gathered below stood in shock. Some were spellbound, others were disappointed that they didn't get to witness what they thought would be a publicized suicide. Investigators searched high and low for any sign of Mr. Globs. It was too big of a stretch to consider that he might actually have gone into an otherworldly portal.

Three Saturdays went by without the children having their storyteller appear to tell them a story. The aura of gloom permeated the entire apartment building. Four weeks passed and the news was still reporting the missing Mr. Globs. The entire city and even 20 other states were glued to the mysterious disappearance of Mr. Globs.

And then, on the fourth Saturday after the event, strange footprints appeared on the sidewalk outside the Belle Aire apartment building. There were two sets — one of a tall man and the other of a finned tail. There was nothing else — only the footprints. And that was just the beginning of the next adventure.

HARRIETTE HOOVER GREEN

As I stood before the entire audience, *I couldn't concentrate, my thoughts finned off into the gloom*, to tomorrow, next year, last week, anything but this moment. *Did I hear him right, did Thomas say what I thought I heard?* I looked around and everyone was staring at me. Damn! Then I saw James down on one knee, holding out a diamond ring toward me.

"Well, what do you say? Will you marry me?"

I nodded my head *yes* and internally thought, *no, no, no!* Everyone applauded. Someone snapped a picture and promised to send it to us. *Pink Martini* played another one of their songs, and the concert continued. Jim rushed me over to where we had been sitting before Thomas, the band's leader, piano player and MC called everyone closer. Jim was smiling ear-to-ear.

"James, you are a clever one," is all I could get out. How could I say *no* in front of all those people? I couldn't embarrass him like that. It is only an engagement, not marriage. *Time will tell. We'll see how it goes, let's not worry over spilled milk*, were the only phrases that came to my mind. I was numb.

He told me we were going to a business gathering in Portland, Oregon from Puyallup, Washington. I was worried I wouldn't give a good impression to his work colleagues. I quizzed him on the names of his business associates and their wives, so I would be able to converse. He answered my questions, but kept saying, "You don't have to worry about that." He did seem a bit distant as we drove to Portland. I assumed he was deep in thought about the gathering and what he needed to accomplish. When he drove up to the theater I saw *Pink Martini* on the billboard. I gasped, "Oh, James! You are too sweet!"

Pink Martini seemed like our own private band we discovered at Bumper Shoots in Seattle. Little did we know they were the rage in Portland and all throughout Europe. They were just one of the performing groups playing on stage at Bumper Shoots. I was totally captivated by the big band sound with percussion galore. There were at least eight different drums and drummers, about five various brass instruments, trumpet, sax, alto sax, french horn, trombone, then violins, bass, viola's — the band was phenomenal! I knew of no other band as big as this. They had around 30 members.

Thomas with his white hair, front bang swooped up in a *hail to the crowd*, was on the piano. He was a singer and was also the MC.

When he introduced Storm, I was hooked. Storm had a voice of enchantment in a deep resonating way. She had a fantastic voice, voluptuous body, very sexy! We were both captivated. *Pink Martini* became our group; we were *groupies*!

"I'm trying to figure out how to get them to play at our wedding," James said as we were driving home to Puyallup. Suddenly an uneasy chill ran up my spine as I realized how good he was at keeping secrets.

"James, however could you keep such a big surprise from me?"

"I nearly told you about it more than once. I just kept thinking about how fun it would be for you to be standing in the audience when Thomas asked if Harriet Hoover Green would marry James Olander." James said.

"You are lucky I didn't faint!"

I sat in silence for several miles as we drove the 150 or so miles back home. I had this uncomfortable feeling that a person who could keep such a big secret could not be fully trusted to be totally honest. Total honesty was one of the core aspects I wanted in a life partner. Total trust, integrity, honesty, good judgement and heart, some of the things John F. Kennedy spoke about when he made his famous *What This Country Needs* speech at his inauguration. That is what I wanted in a partner.

Once home and back in the routine of work, working out, cooking, cleaning and finding time to be together, those thoughts were pushed into the background. Work consumed our weekdays. It was only the weekend when we could be together. Things went along smoothly, but yet there was something nagging in the back of my mind. Every time James said he needed to take a trip for work, I wondered. Every time he was late, or made an excuse to not do the planned thing, I wondered.

Is he telling the truth? *Stop that!* I would tell myself, and eventually I did. As he continued to be loving and generous with gifts and spending money for my pleasure, I stopped wondering. We talked about a wedding, but we seemed content to not firm anything up. What was the rush? There was plenty of time. In fact, a wedding was not really necessary. There would be no children created from the union. It would mean moving in together, and decisions about his house.

My sister came all the way from Michigan to visit. We decided to all go up to Whidbey Island for the weekend to visit Carol Broadway, and stay at Carol Lee's Attic, a really cute Bed & Breakfast. Jim had an unexpected trip to take and begged off. When he called that next morning it was totally unexpected.

"Hello, Jim ... What? ... I don't understand? ... You are asking to be released? ... You are breaking the engagement? ... I don't understand? ... You are going back to your ex-wife? Jim, I don't understand ... Can we talk about this face to face? ... I see, of course, yes, I understand, she needs you more than I."

There was more said that was just yada, yada, yada! He had been obviously communicating with his ex-wife and probably seeing her behind my back, as the saying goes. Tears were swelling in my eyes, wiped away only for more to erupt. My sister asked, "What's wrong?" That question burst the dam.

"Well, he just proved himself to not have those qualities I wanted in a life partner. He lied, several times, no doubt. He could have at least told me they were talking. We aren't two hot-to-trot teens, so in love that there is no reason. I would have been happy to know he was having doubts."

Why didn't I talk with him about my doubts?

All my friends thought he was quite the catch. He fit into my life comfortably, he was a *nice* man. Dating is such a horror. He seemed to really love me. We liked the same lifestyle, music, food, fashion decorating, houses —we were a lot alike, but there wasn't the passion. He didn't have the intensity about life that I had. He didn't ever seem to get very excited about anything. One thing's for sure — he got excited about his *ex* to the point he ended *us.*

KEVIN O'GRADY

The cell walls were thick and damp, too thick to blast a hole through and too damp to lie against. Nonetheless, my mind was racing into all the ways I could escape from the darkness of the black hole I had banished myself to.

I couldn't concentrate, my thoughts finned off into the gloom, and there, like a half developed photograph, I could make out the outline of a doorway.

Was it real or imaginary?, I asked myself, realizing for the first time how isolated I was, and nobody would hear me anyway if I did speak out loud to myself.

Seeing it was the outline of a real door, my inner dialogue stopped just in time before insanity set in, or was I insane to think I was sane in this construct in which I found myself?

Childhood memories were racing through me. Thoughts of how good I'd been as a child, and how terribly awful I'd been also.

Scenes of baby bliss dappled with teenage terror, all played out in the screen of my mind. But one stopped me in my tracks.

I was sitting in an old monastery schoolroom. The teacher was writing in white dusty chalk on an old blackboard. I was reciting out loud each word he wrote, as if he was reaching across the vast infinity of time and space to be with me now.

Stone walls do not a prison make, nor iron bars a cage.

The message was clear as day in the darkness. "I am going mad", I said out loud.

"No, you're not," a voice said from behind the door. "Come this way. Don't be afraid. Remember, stone walls do not a prison make, nor iron bars a cage."

Half expecting some resistance from the thick damp walls, I stepped across the threshold of the imaginary real door, and found myself in an old monastery schoolroom.

"I have been expecting you for a long time," the teacher said in a calm, reassuring manner. He looked the same as he had all those years ago. It was as if I had traveled back in time to my school days, yet I was grown up. I was aware of the passage of over 50 years of time, yet all this was happening right now.

"Who are you?" I asked.

"I am your future self," he said calmly, as if knowing this reply would resurrect the questioning of my own sanity.

"You're not going crazy. It's what you set up for yourself as a child. You yearned for freedom, but you needed to learn what real freedom was first. You needed to experience the power of portals before you could be convinced of your limitlessness."

Just then, someone turned on a light.

"Remove the probes and download the brainwave patterns."

It was my teacher, dressed as a laboratory professor. He was standing under a large green logo of the hemp plant that read, *Accelerated Brainwave Laboratory*. As I drifted off through a doorway into a damp cell, I heard him say, "Next, please."

LINDA KAY

Sitting in a circle of students made up of young professionals led by Dr. Cohen in one of our weekly life improvement sessions, the subject of childhood came up. Up until now, I had been an eager follower of Dr. Cohen's philosophies and ideas, but I felt myself shrink emotionally back into my shell while this topic was discussed. The voices around me became dull, humming sounds and I experienced a tightness in my chest and a desire to get up and leave the room.

The next thing I knew, someone was handing out crayons and brown paper lunch bags. Our teacher was asking everyone to draw a picture of themselves as a child on the flat, folded bag. Then, we were to put our hand inside and pretend it was a hand puppet. Actually, the fold at the bottom of the bag did give one the opportunity to move it up and down like a puppet's mouth.

I sat still, staring at the unmarked bag and unopened box of crayons in my hand. I was getting angry at the idea of having to do such a childish thing.

After all, I paid good money to attend this self-improvement class and felt that this ridiculous task was beneath me. There was no way I could draw myself as a kid. Thinking about it made me sad and very uncomfortable. What was happening to my self-confidence? Why was this exercise causing such a negative reaction? *I couldn't concentrate, my thoughts finned off into the gloom.*

As I watched others around me eagerly drawing faces on the bags, I sat immobilized.

Just seconds away from bolting out of the room, I stopped in my tracks. Something deep inside made me realize that if I had such a strong negative reaction there must be a reason. I decided to stay and find out what it might be.

Slumping begrudgingly back in my chair, I decided not to draw a face on my puppet. Instead, I drew a big yellow flower that reminded me of the fields of yellow mustard weeds around my house where I grew up. I would often lay on my back, feeling the warmth of the earth and gazing through the tall weeds with the bright yellow flowers right above my head. It was a favorite childhood memory.

Finally, Dr. Cohen asked everyone to put down the crayons and slip a hand inside our paper puppets. Reluctantly I slid my hand inside the bag, all the time thinking this was such a stupid exercise. I was determined not to say anything, so no one would know how I felt.

Unfortunately, my resolve to be silent came to a sudden halt as Dr. Cohen instructed us to speak through our puppet when it was our turn. What? Up until now, he had never insisted we speak in the group if we didn't want to. At the very thought, my chest tightened and I experienced a huge lump in my throat that made it hard to breathe.

Much to my dismay, he started with the classmate to his left, leaving me to be the last to say something. There were eighteen students, so I had lots of time for my nervousness to grow. The only rule we were given was that everyone had to say something, even if all we said was our name followed by, "Doesn't want to say anything." I sighed with relief, certainly I could say, "Linda doesn't want to say anything."

It took a while for all the classmates to share their stories from their childhood memories; some happy, some not so happy. The one thing I noticed was no matter what they shared, all I could do was struggle to breathe. The knot in my stomach grew tighter and tighter.

After what seemed to be an eternity, it was my turn. Slowly I held up the paper bag with the yellow flower. With a long pause, and an almost inaudible voice that was being held hostage by my nervousness, the words came out: "Linda says there's no reward in being a kid!"

No! The puppet was supposed to say, Linda doesn't want to say anything!

Instead, the truth had been released from somewhere deep down in the depths of my soul. I had no idea that this was my belief system regarding my childhood. You could hear a pin drop when they heard what my puppet said. Fortunately, Dr. Cohen broke the silence and turned what I'd said into an uplifting message for everyone who had struggled with their childhood.

More importantly, this new information awakened a resolve in me to begin exploring how that belief had affected my life up to now, and it challenged me to make some remarkable changes from that point forward. You might say, that silly paper bag exercise gave me permission to lighten up and not take life so seriously.

A POEM BY DELL BLACKMAN

Caregiver Of Thoughts

And, so ... you want me
To place my wager
Said ... the pessimist
Gazing into the crystal ball
Of course ...
Replied the crystal ball
Just remember ...
The fortunes you project
Will be brought forth
And ... the ones you neglect
Will not appear
For ... you are the caregiver
Of your thoughts.

Prompt #6

I Had Come To NY
To Try Something New

AINGEAL ROSE O'GRADY

I had come to New York to try something new in 1972. New York was always the place to be if you wanted a new life or had an adventurous spirit. It had a reputation of endless opportunity, excitement, glamour and debauchery.

My reasons for coming to New York were simply to jar myself out of the stagnation I had been in for the past 30 years. I was bored. My life had been a tedious routine of rising at dawn, having breakfast, going to my job in a paper mill and returning home at 4 p.m. for the evening. I rarely interacted with anyone outside of my work arena except for the occasional picnics arranged by the company.

Upon reflection, I was aghast at how time had gone by so uneventfully, and now I was in my 50s. *But there was still time,* I thought. *I still had time.*

Selling my possessions was easier than I had anticipated. It was curiosity more than need that brought the villagers to my sale. They wanted to know what the introvert at 64 Banyan St. had kept hidden all these years. I did have quite a collection of rare books, antiques and other collectibles. Seeing 30 years of accumulation gone in a day was a bittersweet experience. The action to get up and go was foreign to my personality. Still, I had to do it. It was do it or die.

The following day I had my ticket and I was on my way. New York it was! While on the journey across the Atlantic, I was surprised that I broke down and cried three quarters of the way. A mixture of emotions had suddenly flooded my mind — the years of working, the solitude and safety of 64 Banyan Street, the familiar people, shops and streets, all were being left behind for a future of strangers and uncertainty.

Still, there was an air of excitement as happens when something entirely new fills the void of what's left behind. The majesty of New York was pure delight. The skyscrapers, the endless rows of shops, streets and houses, the buses and trains, theaters and restaurants filled me with wonder. I was a child again in my 50's.

For the first week I merely watched. Sitting on park benches, on grassy areas by small rivers, in lobbies of fine hotels, in small intimate cafés sipping coffee — I found it all so invigorating. The people were busy, some chatting rapidly with friends while walking to their jobs, others selling papers and food on street corners, and others contemplating within themselves lying on blankets in the park. All of it thrilled me.

How different it was from what I had left behind.

How strange it is that one place can be so secure and predictable, while another place less than a day's journey away can be the total opposite. To find that one decision can lead to an entirely new life, from stagnation to regeneration, was equally as amazing to me. And to see that both places had contained different parts of me made me question time. Had I wasted the past 30 years of my life living the routine, or was it just a stage I was going through? And now, with all this opportunity ahead of me, which facet of myself will I choose to be? I knew for certain that I would not spend another 20 or 30 years doing only one thing. There was too much life to be enjoyed.

So I got myself a sandwich, I fed the pigeons with my crumbs, and I did the only logical next step — I sat down and called my Mother!

CHARLES SCAMAHORN

It was July 1957 and I was just waking up as the truck exited Holland Tunnel into Manhattan. I had been hitchhiking from Pullman, Washington to a summer camp event in New York, called The Encampment for Citizenship, sponsored by the Ethical Culture Society. But what's an 18-year-old college kid doing alone on the highway for a whole week soliciting free rides from passing motorists? It sounds totally crazy! For example, my second ride was with a carload of drunk Indians at 2 AM near Coeur d'Alene, Idaho. Even a foolish kid like me must realize it is dangerous being out on a highway in the middle of the night; anything might happen.

Almost instantly, it seemed, there I was standing blurry-eyed thanking the truck driver and wondering... *what's next?* That exact thought had no doubt entered millions of other people's minds as they first set their foot on Manhattan Island. It was obvious to every one of them, I had come to this place to try something new.

I knew from vague family lore that my first American ancestor, Jacob Janse Schermerhorn, had set his foot on that Manhattan Island back in 1636 as a teenager. He had many adventures from there and from Fort Orange up the Hudson River and from Schenectady, of which he was an early resident. Over the years he developed a thriving fur trade and made several trips back to Amsterdam with beaver pelts. That was certainly adventuresome and every moment of his life was filled with potential disaster. Being out on the sea in a sailing boat is obviously a risk, and trading with Indians for beaver pelts for many years can lead to complex interactions and some instant conflicts with the risk of sudden death. In 1690 Jacob's village of Schenectady was attacked by the French and Indians and many of the residents killed, but his son Simon survived and gave a warning to Fort Orange some fifteen miles away. This is only two years after Jacob wrote his last will and testament, but it isn't known when he died.

Sometime earlier Jacob ended up in jail there in New Amsterdam, put there by the then governor Peter Stuyvesant. The charge was selling guns to Indians. The crime wasn't selling deadly weapons, it was that it was an unwritten law that only Stuyvesant could sell guns to the Indians. That fracas turned out worse for Stuyvesant because the Dutch government said he didn't have the exclusive personal right to sell guns, and thus his jailing of a Dutch citizen was a violation of his authority. He was recalled back to Amsterdam and lost his governorship.

I was vaguely aware of that history, but in an absolutely unexpected turn of events a month after arriving sleepy-eyed in New York I was talking to the former first lady of the United States, Eleanor Roosevelt, at her home in Hyde Park when she said, "Charles, you know we are related." I almost fainted, and literally ran away! *I had come to New York to try something new*, but this was far and away too much.

Six decades later I still get the willies thinking about my New York adventure.

HARRIETTE HOOVER GREEN

He was feeling excited at all the sights and sounds of the people moving in waves as they all walked down the sidewalk in unison. The various colors of clothing, the different faces, the fact that they moved together; how thrilling!

His mind went to the time, 9:00 a.m. He would not be late for his appointment for the interview. Everything was going smoothly, he felt good about this idea of moving to New York to have a big change in his life. He felt assured this was the direction to go at this stage in his life; a fresh start.

His mind ran through the list of things he wanted to include in the interview; his contributions to his last school, his promotions and his desire for a greater challenge in his work, more responsibility, and why he was confident this job would be the perfect job for him, and he the perfect candidate.

He felt a surge of energy filling his body as he thought of the possibilities. Head of the Psychology Department at Antioch, New York, perfect!

This was a big responsibility, but absolutely what he was looking for. Antioch was a very progressive university based on wide open consciousness. The classes were based on non-stereotypical thought, Couples and Family Therapy versus Marriage and Family Therapy as degree programs. Marriage was not necessary for a couple to be together. Couples could be of the same sex. They also offered a non-graded way of measuring the students knowledge of the course curriculum. All assessing is done on a completed paper, addressing the information given throughout the entire semester; no testing, no memorizing, only *knowing* based on demonstrated knowledge reflected in the end-of-term paper.

The room was filled with tastefully selected furniture in a calming color for a relaxed interview. The faces around the table were welcoming and smiling warmly. "Good morning," he said as he stretched out his hand toward the nearest person. Each person introduced themselves and stated their position at the University. He shook hands all around and then said, "My name is James, James W. Tompkins. I hope to be your new Director of the Psychology Department. *I had come to NY to try something new*, working in a city instead of the more rural environment I've had the past 10 years. That environment lulled me into a sort of malaise. I want excitement, fast paced energy all around me to charge my batteries and get the creative juices flowing. I have some ideas I need to hone before I present them to the board, but first I will demonstrate I am able to run the Department the way it is before I suggest making any changes. Be assured, I intend to introduce a totally new, innovative concept of learning the art of psychological treatment, or counseling, more in line with the newest science of recognizing we are intuitive creatures able to intuit from each other without verbiage. Just like I am understanding I have your full attention." At this point, he sat down expecting questions. There was a huge silence and the faces around the table looked surprised by his sudden silence and decision to sit.

Just then someone laughed, then another and another as the interviewers understood they had all come to the same conclusion, *He was their man!* They felt it in their entire bodies, not just their minds. This felt more right than any of them had ever experienced. Mrs. Nottingham broke the silence and said, "How did you do that? Were we hypnotized?" Now James laughed and said, "No, you just allowed your intuition to speak to your being." The group then started talking amongst themselves, smiling and laughing in a very relaxed manner. The mood was festive, nothing like anyone had experienced in an interview. *He was magical,* he heard someone say. His excitement and self assuredness had flowed into their field and they were in the same vibration of excitement with the possibilities for their University.

If his ideas work in the psychology department, then they may work school wide. Antioch, New York would be the only school using this unique teaching style. They would then become even more famous for their innovative concepts and stand out as being an exceptional school everyone will want to attend.

This new consciousness is mind boggling. Hah, that is an understatement! It is opening a whole new way to think, a whole new way to be, a whole new way to be in community; a way to feel alive! James felt assured he would be offered the job. Just think, this all came about just because he decided to come to New York to try something new!

Kevin O'Grady

My mind raced back to the days of the potato famine in Ireland. I could see the starving people dying in the fields and in the streets with no hope of food and no hope for the future. I thought how delicate our lives really are, how our very existence hangs by the thread of a single breath in each moment.

I had come to New York to try something new, but whatever it was going to be, it seemed to be interminably linked to my ancestral past. Was it justice I was seeking, or was it simply survival? Was I looking to thrive, or was I destined to reenact the starvation of the past?

I stared at the old brick warehouse and thought how cynical, how amusing it would be to turn this abandoned grain store into my own Irish music venue. I could sing about the famine but not relive it. I could honor all the tragic deaths but not enter into their pain. I could write music that felt their hunger but never have to experience their emptiness. That day I called some banks to get a loan.

"But you have no money in your account," they said, one after another. Each refusal from the banks sent shocking reminders through the dark corridors of my ancestral memory. "No Irish need apply." I began to feel the despair of the homeless, the uselessness of the outcast, the agony of the starving, and the rush of determination from my family line.

Someone of my family must've survived, otherwise I would not be here. Someone of my people must've said, no to death by hunger. Someone of my lineage must've said, I will do it. I will live.

I watched a taxi stop opposite the warehouse doors. In the same instant, in my mind's eye, I saw an ancestor of mine open the big wooden doors and feed people from the huge store of food inside. As I floated between the two worlds of starvation and plenty, I watched the man pay the taxi driver then wrap his silk scarf around his neck to protect from the cold east wind blowing up the Hudson from Ellis Island.

All the windows were boarded up so I couldn't see what he was doing inside, but there was a broken board beside a rusty drain pipe that gave me the vantage point I needed.

I wiped the years of grime from the glass and waited while my eyes adjusted to the dim light inside. He seemed to be measuring something. He paced up and down and right to left, avoiding the steel supports that held up the four aged oak floors above.

Suddenly, my drain pipe broke and I crashed down on the concrete pavement to a swirl of stars.

"Hey, are you a musician?" I could hear the voice as if it was a long way off into the distance.

"Yes, I am," I said, wiping the blood from my forehead.

"Then play for me, and I'll feed you and I'll take you with me on the ship to America."

My mind slipped effortlessly between the two realities. In one, I was being helped aboard an immigrant ship bound for America, and in another reality I was being helped up from the pavement outside an old grain store on New York's east side.

"Come in out of the cold," the man said. "Let me tell you my plans for this warehouse." He looked at me as if he could see right into my heart's desires. His words were comforting and reassuring, and I felt he either knew me from someplace in America, or he knew me from Ireland. *Was he related to me in some way?*

"I am looking for a partner," he continued, "a musician to turn this old storehouse into an Irish music venue. We will have a history section depicting the Irish famine upstairs, and stores on the other levels selling Irish linen and woolen goods and Irish musical instruments. In this huge area over there we will have the most famous Irish music venue in all of America!"

As I signed the contract for our building, I couldn't help but notice how remarkably similar my new partner looked to my great, great grandfather.

LINDA KAY

I had come to New York to try something new. No, not to seek fame and fortune; just to refresh and regroup and put the past behind me. It seemed important to get as far away as I could from my sordid history, including people, places and bad intentions. New York was the furthest place I could get to with my limited resources. Had I had the financial means, the Caribbean would have been my preferred choice. That was not going to happen, so I chose the highway.

After the last of a series of unfortunate and life-sucking mishaps, I barely had money to buy a loaf of day-old bread and some off-brand peanut butter. There was no family to call or friends to count on. I had severed those bonds years ago when I left my hometown in a flurry of broken relationships and bad debts.

Why had I been unable to see through the dust of my self-destruction and alcohol abuse? Why didn't I listen to the pleadings from friends and family who tried to intervene and steer me in a new direction?

What had gone so wrong? If I had stolen money from anyone but my parents I would have surely ended up in jail. Unfortunately, they were both gone now and I will never have the chance to thank them for putting up with me over the years. It is a sobering thought to realize that there is no one in my corner to cheer me on or encourage me. I have made such a mess of things that I am sure even God has given up on me; if there really is a God.

If it had not been for ending up at the Reno Gospel Mission hoping for a hot meal and a place to sleep for the night, I may not have made this journey. Everything I had in the world had been taken from me while hitchhiking. How could I have known that the two guys who offered me a ride just east of Reno would beat me up and take the few belongings I had left? Looking back, it is surprising they didn't take the clothes I was wearing before dumping me out in the desert.

For my twenty-three years on the planet, that experience was one of the lowest points in my life; ending up at the Gospel Mission ran a close second.

That night at the Mission, a guy gave some kind of sermon before the food was served. I don't recall much about what he said over the gurgling and growling of my empty stomach that was aching for food, but one thing he said stuck with me big time. He told our motley group of street-worn and outcast men that the next time we looked in a mirror, or saw a reflection of ourselves in a store window, the face we saw was the face of the person who put us where we were.

While the message was tough to hear, it became the motivating factor that brought me to New York hoping to begin a new chapter in my life. This time, the new beginning starts with me taking responsibility for myself and my actions. Hopefully, I can do things differently, so that the face looking back at me in the mirror, will be the face of the person who helped me build a better life for myself.

A Poem By Dell Blackman

Resting At Home

The pale in my reflection
doesn't tell the story
The lines on my face
don't lead anywhere
All that's left
is the journey
traveled
through these eyes
And, the comfort
they now feel
resting at home.

Prompt #7

Just Who Will You Be?

AINGEAL ROSE O'GRADY

Today was the first day of the rest of her life. She had completely lost her memory. She had woken up like that and found herself on a beach to the sound of the ocean lapping softly against her feet. Gulls were squawking in the air overhead. It was too early for any beachcombers to arrive. She sat up and looked around. The sun was just beginning to rise. The moon was still in its place with a faint glow of stars overhead. Faint sparkles of light were beginning to dance on the peaceful water and she suddenly became aware of herself in this pristine place. Where was she and how did she get here?

She thought it odd that she wasn't cold in the brisk early morning air. Her legs and feet were sandy, her cotton printed skirt was damp as was her hair and her light blue top. She had no recollection of how she got here; she had obviously slept here or so she assumed.

Suddenly, she realized she had no memory of being anyone. The realization made her begin to panic. She stood up, brushed herself off and walked to the first street she saw just a few blocks away.

Small quaint cottages began to appear — the kind you'd find in New England. Breakfast cafés were just opening and the aroma of fresh brewed coffee filled her nostrils. She entered one called, *The Salty Sea* and she asked the small gray haired woman behind the counter where she was.

"Why, you're in the state of Maine, in the United States of America."

The only thing that was obvious to her was that she spoke English. The woman, whose name was Gretchen, offered her a complimentary cup of coffee and a freshly made breakfast of eggs, bacon and homemade bread.

Now what? she thought.

She had asked Gretchen if she recognized her, or ever saw her before and her answer was, *"No"*. After her breakfast, she walked the sandy downtown streets, asking others in shops and on sidewalks if they recognized her and their answers were always, "no". A kind man of about forty took her to the local police station where she could inquire into any missing person reports. Nothing had been reported. No one had been looking for her.

Bewildered and still frightened, she made her way again to the beach. By now it was early afternoon, the sun was warm and the beach was now populated with sunbathers and swimmers. As she stared at the glistening ocean, a flash of being somewhere else briefly entered her mind.

What was that? she thought. It was something about the way the sun hit the water — the mixture of light and motion triggered what appeared to be a memory, a glimpse, a window. She stared at the water again, hoping for another trigger. A dolphin appeared on the surface as if to say, "Hello". Her vision went to scenes of swimming underneath the water into the depths, down through algae and coral and marine life of all kinds. *Could it be? Do I dare? No, not yet.*

So, who would she be if she could be anyone? *Just who will you be?* she mused to herself.

She'd be free. Free to be anyone in any moment — changeable, spontaneous and unlimited. No memory of the past or of anything that had gone before, but only *now*. Being in the *now*, the fullness of the moment, fully embodied. Being and embracing and then, just then, as suddenly as she had appeared on that moist sandy beach, she disappeared into the foam.

CHARLES SCAMAHORN

Never have I been asked, *"Just who will you be?"*

I know who I am now, and who I will be in a hundred years is obvious. I will be dead and long gone and probably long forgotten. Perhaps something I did or wrote will be remembered — probably not. I am now old, so whoever it is that I am going to become will soon be known to me, but only when I get there.

That being the probable situation, and I being who I am, I will probably still be me. And I will still be recognizable to myself and others. My personality has been drifting toward getting grumpier but I am trying to create the habit of being kinder; kinder to other people and kinder to myself too.

If I am successful in creating that habit in a few years, I will be a noticeably kinder and a less grumpy person. Nowadays when I see people do stupid things, I still get grumpy, and when I see it's me thinking stupid thoughts I get grumpy with myself. When I see it's me that's doing stupid things I get super grumpy.

So, who will I be, say, in five years? A sweet, kindly

old man? Or an obnoxious geriatric crank? The way it's going at the moment the most likely *me* t'will be... uh, both. When I am confronted with a situation that I am comfortable with I will be the kind, funny old guy, but when I am involved in a bit of human stupidity I will react with the wimpy sarcasm of a feeble old fool.

Sarcasm is a trait I was infamous for in my teens so, as I revert through the aging process back into geriatric infancy, I will probably go through a sarcastic period. Some of my friends probably already think I'm sarcastic but it can get worse, but, if that reversion to childhood continues, in ten years at age ninety-one I will become a cute kid again. A kid that young mothers will coddle, and hopefully, kindly old ladies will feed chocolate chip cookies and milk to.

I don't remember being kind as a little kid. I do remember wondering why the other kids were mean and my not participating in their meanness, but intentionally being kind, by seeing into other people's problems and helping them work through those problems... well, that's a bit advanced for a child.

Perhaps, for a geriatric man, reverting toward old-age infancy, it may be possible to be intentionally kind. So, perhaps, just perhaps, in my last few years on Earth rather than in it I will become a kind old man.

And perhaps when asked "Who was he?" people will say of me, like Hamlet said of his dead father, "He was a man. Take him complete, with all his flagrant faults exposed. He was a man!"

HARRIETTE HOOVER GREEN

In the land of Shreshrena just who will you be is never a question; you will be a warrior! Everyone becomes a warrior. Once you turn 12 and are into your full flower, the training begins whether you want to or not. All must serve. Age 12 is when your body begins to bloom into its full development. The training is very physical and your body will grow strong muscles. The body will morph from thin to thick, frail to strong, child to adult. The sweet essence of a child no more. From loving to fierce, ready to kill whomever you are told to kill.

Ariellia has kept her secret for one plus years, having stolen bits and pieces of cloth and furs she uses to catch the bleed. She would wash them at the water's edge, hanging them to dry high in her friend the Grandfather tree. She knew her friend would not betray her. They communicated by touching together their *knowing*.

Deep in the earth, through the roots, from tree to tree, up through the earth to Ariellia, making her at one with all plant life. It was her Grandfather tree who suggested the plan. He knew she was not meant to be a warrior. She felt very special to have discovered she could communicate with the trees and plants, animals and birds and knew how to read the thoughts of another without words. This had alway been so for Ariellia, as far back as she could remember; back to when her mother was with her, before her death from an accidental fall off a high cliff. One minute she was there, the next gone. Ariellia was six years old by their count method; Marco was a baby whom she cared for until the Shreshrena found them and took them in and cared for them knowing they would have two more warriors in time.

Once her bleed is discovered by her familiar group, she will be moved to the Familiar House and the teachings of how to be a Shreshrena will begin. Her mother, Arcnella, told her to never forget that she had special abilities given for her soul purpose. She was an Achtennaagen. Her mother told Ariellia her story over and over how she, Arcnella and Dunoc, Ariellia's mother and father joined the Shreshrena when their entire village were killed or run off when the two were sent to look for food. Only Arcnella and Dunoc survived. They decided to assimilate with the Shreshrena or face certain death of a most unpleasant manner.

Ariellia thought, *I am not a Shreshrena, I am an Achtennaagen. I am special, I have special abilities, I have knowings.* She then spoke this aloud, "It is so for me and Marco, it is so also for you!" As the siblings were exchanging thoughts, sitting close, trying to decide how to prevent Ariellia from attending the warrior school, the warning horn sounded loudly. It meant immediate threat. The two rushed off to the bluff to observe the village. The warriors had gathered together and were donning their armor and gathering their weapons.

"Look Marco, those ships fly our people's flag. Look, that is the cloth mother had you wrapped in. It was used by the Familiar Mothers for your first shirt. We must warn them. Our people are not all killed. They are special like you and me. We share the same abilities. This is good!"

Together they sat in a meditation pose sending a warning signal to their people, telling them they will be attacked if they leave their ship. Telling them to leave for now and meditate on the dilemma. Any hope of joining them now was useless. Ariellia and Marco must send out their thoughts and knowings to their people for a peaceful joining. That is it! She remembered her mother's words exactly.

"You have gifts for your soul purpose."

"Exactly! Marco, we are here to teach these people. That is our soul purpose, we are here to open the hearts of the Shreshrena. This must be so!"

They scurried down the bluff running toward the head fighter, Gurdo. He was shouting orders to all around them, while Ariellia yelled, "Wait, wait, I must speak to you!" He shoved her away but she pushed back grabbing a sword as she charged back toward him. That action startled him and he stopped in his tracks.

"What are you doing? You are still a child. You have not had the training."

Ariellia said, "I have something that is so much better. I want to share it with you."

Gurdo said, "Then be quick."

Ariellia then proceeded to read his mind and report what he was thinking to the smallest detail.

"You are a witch," Gurdo said in amazement. Ariellia then read another warrior's mind, and another and another. There was total silence as the enormity of her abilities sunk into their minds.

"How do you do that?", Gurdo asked.

Ariellia explained it was her soul purpose to teach people of all lands to do this and end war altogether! By this time someone had brought the elders and the healers to hear Areillia speak. The elders were impressed with her abilities and began talking amongst themselves.

"There was a story of a people who had these skills, but I didn't believe it was true."

They thought, with this knowledge we can conquer the world!

"No!" said Ariellia, "With this knowledge you can provide peace over all the lands, between all peoples, no more war, warriors no longer dying, and for that you will be famous throughout the entire land and beyond! Instead of dead warriors, you will be famous for ending all wars, and the land will live in peace and prosperity. In case that is not enough of an incentive, I will give you another good reason not to attack them."

With that statement Ariellia grabbed Gurdo's sword, which was bigger than she and with expert precision she swung the sword, stopping it at Gurdo's neck, to the shock and gasp of the people, as well as Gurdo.

She said, "I was born with superior skills as a warrior, plus the ability to read your mind. I know what you plan to do as soon as you think it. This is a good day for the Shreshrena, they can live in peace with all of mankind. Do you not realize these men on the ship have these skills, you would not have a chance if you chose to fight them."

Before Gurdo could respond, a horn alerted the crowd's attention back to the ship in the harbor.

"These are my people." Ariellia said. "We are from Achtennaagen. We all share the same abilities. I think we should welcome them with open arms. What do you say Gurdo? What do you say, Shamon? What do you say Elder Ones, *just who will you be?*"

The lock clicked shut, signaling a kind of finality to what just happened. A mere five minutes before, Maria Delarosa had been in total confusion over what she would do with her life. Now it was as clear as the fresh waters that cascaded down from the Pyrenees that lay to the north of her village.

She had just brought her herd of Spanish sheep and goats down from the high pastures in preparation for the onset of winter. In many ways, she felt this area of the Basque region of northern Spain perfectly reflected her life. She felt small in a small village. She felt unknown and irrelevant in the vastness of the great Pyrenees that effectively separated the Basque region from all of Spain, from France, and Mainland Europe.

Like her native people, she felt marginalized and isolated in the bigger scheme of the world stage, but most of all, the part she dreamed of playing was never presented to her.

Her long black hair cascaded down her shoulders just like the mountain rivers, and her fine, high cheekbones and perfect skin could have her on the catwalks of the famous fashion houses of Paris, or New York, or on the movie sets of Hollywood.

As she sat in the village tavern resting from her hard day on the mountains, a stranger with a strong Italian accent offered her a place in his forthcoming movie called, *Love In A Faraway Place*. The film crew was arriving in a week and the tavern would become their location headquarters.

"Just who will you be?" the Italian asked, as he sampled the famous sangria of the region. He paused, and again repeated it, as if saying it a second time would bring some kind of clarity to his need for a special leading lady.

"*Just who will you be?*"

Maria's mind was racing. *What will my father say? What will happen when my boyfriend finds out I spent the afternoon in the back office of the tavern with an Italian movie mogul?*

Then her self-doubts kicked in. She was familiar with the lines she constantly told herself.

You're no good. You're a loser. You're just an ugly duckling of a shepherd, a lowly goat-herder.

But there was a difference in everything this time. Before, she was always alone on the mountain with only her own voice to listen to, and she was tired of the same old back-chatter telling her she would never be the singer or the actress she always wanted to be. But now, the director wanted her to play the leading part. She would sing, and dance, and wine and dine in style as the leading lady. She would also be the lover in, *Love In A Faraway Place.*

She stood with her back to the locked door. Behind her, in her tiny bedroom, lay all her worldly possessions. In the pocket of her long handmade dress was her ticket to freedom, her passport to fame and fortune.

"Just who will you be?" the director had asked her. "I will be myself," she said, "I will be loyal to my boyfriend, and take care of my father in his old age, and I will continue to attend my sheep and my goats."

Suddenly, a shot rang out from inside the room. The bullet ripped through the door, sending splinters in a thousand directions. It left a neat hole in the back of Maria's dress, and blood ran down through the cracks of the old tavern floor. Marie's deep black eyes turned up to heaven, and closed slowly. The last sound heard in that scene was the delighted voice of her newly promoted boyfriend shouting, "Cut!"

Sam Carter was one of Maggie's best friends. Knowing her as well as he did, it came to no surprise when his younger brother, Randy, announced that he was going to ask her to marry him. Caught a little off guard, Sam said, "So that's why you asked me to drop you off at the Auto Repair Shop to pick up your car. When did all this happen?"

"I've been thinking about it for days," answered Randy.

They both sat quietly studying the traffic ahead. Randy waited for more of a reaction. Sam pretended to have his mind on the traffic as he searched through his memory for Maggie-related information. If anyone could pull Randy out of his year of post-divorce doldrums, it was Maggie. She could turn a stone man to putty with her infectious smile. She could also leave your life as quickly as she came into it.

Playing the protective role of the older brother, Sam cautiously cut into the silence and asked, "Randy, have you ever given Maggie a box of chocolates?"

Sam didn't have to take his eyes off the road to know that Randy shot him one of those, *What are you talking about?* looks.

He patiently repeated the question. Then Randy said, "No. Why? She doesn't eat that stuff anyway."

"Once in a while she does," answered Sam. "But, that is not the point. I watched her once. First, she goes after her favorites, the milk-chocolate-covered nuts. They're easy to spot. Then, not wanting to miss something she may like, Maggie uses the point of a sharp knife and opens a spot in the bottom of each of the other candies to see what is inside. If it looks good to her, she eats it. If not, she puts it back for someone else to have."

Randy instinctively knew his brother was leading to something. They didn't spend much time together as adults, but Randy had been listening to Sam's dissertations since they were kids. He could feel it coming.

"Okay, what's your point, big brother?"

"Well," hesitated Sam, "that's kind of the way Maggie enjoys men. She checks them all out, and then goes after her favorites." Holding up his right hand to delay Randy's comeback, he added, "Now, before you say anything, remember she is one of my best friends. I have known her for twelve years, and I love her like a sister. But, you are my brother, and I just want to be sure you know what you are doing. If nothing else, look at her track record. She is 36 years old and has had a four year affair that outlasted her marriage, not to mention a number of short-lived relationships. Maggie is like an incredible magnet. Guys are instinctively drawn to her and they always want to marry her. She truly likes men. That's why I can't see her settling down with just one guy for any permanent relationship, even if it is with my brother."

Randy cut in, "Are you sure this isn't just sour grapes or something? How come you never got past a platonic friendship with Maggie?"

Sam took his time to answer as his mouth slowly broadened into a knowing smile as he said, "Because her friendships outlast her relationships. I guess I like having Maggie in my life, and one way to keep her there is to just be her friend. Besides, I want to be married someday, and marriage is not for Maggie. I think of her as a butterfly; once captured, she will wither and die. I'd rather see her flitting about from flower to flower, so to speak," he added, cringing at his own metaphor, "at least that way, her unique, emancipated spirit will last."

Pulling into the repair shop parking lot, Sam turned slightly in his seat to look directly at his brother. "Look, I care about you and I care about Maggie. She is wonderful, and I have no doubt you two would be very happy for a while. However, you've only been divorced about a year, so why rush into anything? I really don't want to see you become one of her statistics."

Randy remained very quiet while his brother continued, "Please realize I'm not trying to butt into your business, however, I know Maggie. Whether she marries you or not, she probably won't stay with you. Sooner or later she will move on. *Just who will you be* a few years from now, a husband or an ex-husband?"

Randy's face was flushed and he could feel the anger growing as he asked Sam, "How do you know that will happen? You could be wrong. People change. You make it sound so hopeless. I love her and I want to marry her. How can you sit there telling me what a rotten idea this would be? What do you expect me to say?"

"Say, yes, or say, no, it's up to you," replied Sam. "Maybe you don't have to make that decision today. Just don't make the mistake of talking marriage until you are sure you can live with the results."

"Okay, Sam, I hear you. But, if what you say is true, that Maggie will leave sooner or later, maybe I want to take my chances. You said yourself that having her in your life is better than not having her at all. Remember, Sam, you are the same guy who told me when I got divorced, that there were no guarantees in life."

With that, Randy got out of the car and walked around to the driver's side to say goodbye to Sam. He noticed a yellow dandelion flowering at his feet, and bent down and broke it off at the base of its stem. Handing it to Sam through the open window, he said,

"Here, big brother, you are now holding my fate. Should I ask Maggie to marry me or shouldn't I? Pick off one petal at a time. The first one is 'yes,' the second is 'no' and the third one is 'maybe.' Continue in that order until you get to the last petal. Then, call and leave a message to let me know the answer. I'll be out with your good friend, Maggie."

Like No Other

Our choices
are the dancers
on the floor
of destiny
And, when ...
the movements
are graceful
led by steps
of compassion
It's a spectacle
like no other.

Prompt #8

More Than One Winter Has Found
Me Working In A Silver City Dive
That Beckons To The Thirsty With
A Classic Neon Sign Of A Cactus
In The Foreground And A
Horseman Drifting Alone
Into The Distance

AINGEAL ROSE O'GRADY

It's not easy being on the road. Thumbing rides across country has its pros and cons. On lucky days, my thumb provides me a ride lasting three or more hours towards my destination with a good driver and conversational companion. Down days consist of a series of short spurts with hours going by in-between. Occasionally I find myself destined to stay days on end in locations not of my choosing due to severe weather or other unforeseen circumstances.

More than one winter has found me working in a Silver City dive that beckons to the thirsty with the classic neon sign of a cactus in the foreground and a horseman drifting alone into the distance.

Ironically, these places give me a smorgasbord of patron delights. People from across the world find themselves in these places, grateful for a cup of coffee and a breakfast of eggs, grits, bacon and sausage.

I love the early mornings. I love the aromatic smell of coffee and bacon, seeing the sunrise and welcoming the day. It's the breakfast crowd that piques my interest. They have the best stories and are usually ready to give you all the details from thrills to spills.

One of my favorites was Jessie's story. She was an elderly woman, well-worn with experiences. The kind of eyes that still sparkle with life even though the outer skin reveals the years. Jessie was also a traveler like myself. She had been years on the road, much more than I. She had been across the US several times, hitchhiking and walking most of the way. By now she was well known on the highways by her well worn boots, blue cotton shirt and colorful hat. And if you still weren't sure it was her, the cigar hanging out of her mouth was a dead giveaway.

Jessie's favorite adventure began when she had just been let off a ride in the mountains of Colorado. It was springtime and the streams were full of music. Times like these were Jessie's favorites. She would camp out beneath pines on the edges of some stream and stay there for days. This particular day, Jessie found herself edging towards a large opening in a cliff wall. It beckoned her with some familiar calling. As she approached, the coolness and darkness of the large cave made her pause, but only for a moment. She was an adventurer after all! She lit a small candle tucked inside her jacket pocket for just such an occasion. A small breeze caused the candle flame to flicker, but Jessie continued on. The cave was large, extending many lengths back into darkness. Jessie sat on a large rock that jutted out and hung over a ledge.

Had she not stopped here to rest, she would've found herself tumbling down thousands of feet into a large crevice that led to a deep river below.

Sounds of tiny birds could be heard some distance away, too far for Jessie to follow. Jessie realized she could go no further and stood up to go back. As she did, her candle flame died out leaving her with no light and no way to know which way lead back to the opening. She felt for her box of matches in her jacket pocket, but to her surprise there were none there. She must've lost them somewhere along the way, she thought. This would be a test of her senses which were already heightened due to the raw reality of where she was and where she had to go. She knew if she was not out of the cave by nightfall, she could easily be compromised by rapid cooling temperatures and a lack of food and water.

Backing away from the rock, she began to tread carefully. This time she was keenly aware of every step — twigs crackling under her worn boots and thin slices of rock breaking in rows. By now the confusion of direction was upon her. She did not know which way to turn. After a few moments of deliberation, she did the only thing she could do. She turned herself into a bird and flew away.

HARRIETTE HOOVER GREEN

Her perfume wafted into his nostrils with a titillating aroma. "Can I buy you a drink?", he asked with a smiling face. She turned toward him on her bar stool and thought briefly as she assessed him. "That would be okay." The bartender took her order and brought her a Side Car. She sipped the drink and sat quietly, waiting for him to say something; he clearly wanted company.

"My name is John Carleton. May I ask your name?" She answered giving him a fake name, Ginger Houseman. "Well, Ginger, what brings you here? You look out of place."

She was dressed in an expensive pair of slacks and matching top with high heels. Definitely not the attire for a dusty, broken down town and a cheap saloon.

"My car broke down and is being repaired. How about yourself? I could say the same about you." John explained he was a traveling salesman and just got tired of driving, saw the cactus sign and decided to get a drink, a bite to eat and crash in the motel for the night.

She asked what he sold and where he was headed and other mundane bits of information as she continued to feel him out. They chatted for a while, he bought her another Side Car and then asked her if she would be willing to have dinner with him there in the bar, or wherever she liked. She said, "This is about as good as it gets here." He apologized for the informal setting and said, "But in your company this will be perfect."

She was beginning to feel the buzz from the alcohol, which also gave her the sense of confidence she needed to proceed. No matter how many johns she turned, she was always a bit uneasy in the assessing part of the contact. Especially after the big mistake she made in the past.

He was clearly not a cop. She had his name, where he lived and his story. He was an ordinary guy, doing a lonely job away from his family and stuck in this god-forsaken place. She felt this would be a safe one. After they finished eating, she leaned forward and asked if he had ever paid for sex while he was traveling.

"Why would you ask me that?", he said with a surprised look on his face.

"I wondered if you would like to pay for my time tonight. It is one price for just the sex and another price for the entire night."

At that, he sat back in his chair in silence and awe. He thought about her question, shook his head back and forth, then leaned forward and asked in a whisper,

"Are you in trouble? You can't mean you are a prostitute. Are you working for someone? Ginger, tell me your story." She pushed her chair back, thanked him for the drinks and the meal and started to get up from her chair when he lightly grabbed her arm, saying, "Please tell me why you are doing this?"

"Good night John, it was nice spending time with you." She rose to leave.

"Wait, wait, okay. I'll pay you to spend the night. What will that cost?"

"$300.00," she said.

"What, in this town, really?"

"If you aren't happy I will return your money," she said with a smile.

He shook his head in amazement, thinking this can't be happening. Maybe she was trying to get him busted for buying sex. He was in a dilemma, he was out of his comfort zone by a million miles! He felt for this woman, and didn't know what would have caused her to service men in this way; it was such a dangerous profession. He knew of friends who had indulged in paid sex, but he had not. It wasn't sex he wanted, it was understanding. Ginger had an air about her. She was mysterious, sensuous, classy, educated, and not a woman who would be turning tricks in a cheap bar in a dumpy town.

"Where shall we go?", he asked. She explained the arrangements and asked for the money in the bar. Again he was surprised, thinking he didn't think that was the way it was usually done, but still determined to find out what was causing this woman to act this way. He said, "Wait, I need another drink before we leave."

She sat back down and now leaned back in her chair and was visibly relaxed. They ordered another drink and he asked her again to explain her reasons or at least tell him about herself. *He paid for the night*, she thought, *talking without sex would be nice. More than one winter has found me working in a Silver City dive that beckons to the thirsty with a classic neon sign and a horseman drifting alone into the distance, that's Vegas!*

John asked, "How old were you when you began this work?" Ginger explained that her parents were killed in an auto accident when she was 16. She was in shock for a while and just dropped out of school, not being able to concentrate or do her assignments. No one seemed to notice. They weren't close to the neighbors, being new to the area. Her dad had just started a new job and her mom was still looking when the accident happened. The police said they were hit by a drunk driver head o and were killed instantly. Someone from the police department helped get her parents cremated. There was no funeral, no caskets. When it was over she was still numb. It felt like a bad dream that she would wake from and be back in school with her parents at their place and home.

Tears rolled down her face as she told her story. There was no money for her to continue to live in the apartment. Once it was all gone and she was evicted, she decided she would hitch a ride to Reno to see if she could get a job as a server.

She did get a job as a server and enjoyed it. She did it well. Things were going along well and she was saving money when she had an emergency appendicitis. The bills wiped out her savings. She lost her job because she wasn't able to work. Once she was well, she needed money badly. Sleeping on the streets of Reno was not safe. She told herself she would do *it* just once and then get another job serving and train to be a dealer in a casino. Once she was good enough she would move from Reno to Vegas.

Things didn't go smoothly. The man she had for her first trick beat her up, ending her back in the hospital. More bills and no money, she felt she had to make money fast and turning tricks was fast money, not easy, but fast. She said, "I eventually became numb during the act. I turned my mind toward the heavens and pretended this was the way to become an angel. Many of the men are so wounded, so alone, so sad that I feel I am giving them the love they've needed all their lives. They are often misfits. You, John are out of the norm. I ended up here when my car broke down. I need the money to pay for the car repair. I'll be headed home once it is done. You John, are a nice man."

John handed her $500 cash, his bonus for this quarter that he had just received, and said, "Hearing your story and being able to help you, is all I need."

Ginger said, "Thank you, Angel, my heart is full."

KEVIN O'GRADY

Solomon kicked the empty beer bottle to the sandy curb, startling the horses that were tied to the wooden handrail under the neon sign. Everything seemed out of place — the bottle, the sandy streets, the neon sign, even his name was foreign in these parts. His fingers caressed the handle of the Colt 45 that slung loosely around his waist, his keen eyes taking in every movement of the gang members in front of the new saloon.

Tombstone City had welcomed him initially, as it did all newcomers. But the Harley gang quickly took a dislike to his name. It was too Biblical, they said. It reminded them of how violent they were, of how far they had strayed from the message of peace that he preached. *More than one winter has found me working in a Silver City dive that beckons to the thirsty with a classic neon sign of a cactus in the foreground and a horseman drifting alone into the distance.*

But it was that lone horseman that would determine whether Solomon would live or die that January day.

Everything about the place was cold. The steel handle of his gun was cold. The sharp air blowing up from the desert was cutting into his nostrils, down into his chest. He felt the air itself was making his heart cold to what he had to do.

Watching from the safety of my saloon, I pleaded mentally with Solomon to not go any further. I begged in my minds eye for him not to turn the corner onto Main Street. From my vantage point, I could see how much the Harley gang outnumbered him. I could see through his cold black eyes, unflinching in the steely air, unaccustomed to mercy.

Suddenly, a horseman galloped to the saloon and dismounted, tying his gray stallion to the rail beside the other horses, their whinnying distracting the Harley gang just enough for Solomon to draw first. One Harley brother fell to the ground. Another ran behind a hay bale. Another ducked behind the water trough. The horseman, thinking they were firing at him, drew his Winchester Repeater from his saddle, and within seconds four men lay dead on the sandy windswept street. Seeing the danger was now over, I pushed through the swing doors of my saloon to greet the horseman. But thinking I was another of the gang, his reaction was swift and decisive. His last round found its mark in my heart, taking me to the ground instantly. As the world blurred around me, I watched my blood run through the cracks of the boardwalk to be quickly soaked up by the cold sand below. I could hear the words coming from my right. It was Solomon whispering in my ear, "May God bless you," I could hear him say, "and may Our Lord Jesus Christ take you to sit on the right hand of the Father."

Suddenly, I felt someone kick me in the ribs. It was the horseman.

"Get up you drunken fool. I don't pay you to drink my beer. I employ you to serve my customers. Now serve my good friend Solomon and I your very best Neon Classic Cactus Western Pale Ale."

The winter had been harsh and unforgiving with bitter cold temperatures and howling winds. Unfortunately, Mother Nature had affected the normal flow of visitors to Silver City with their high hopes of finding some unhidden fortune in the depths of deserted gold mines that dotted the landscape of this tiny mountain town.

Why they called this place Silver City was a wonder since the gold rush was actually responsible for bringing a motley assortment of hardy hopefuls to the area, populating the tiny town. Most had left once they realized there was little gold in the area. The town was so small it did not deserve to be called a city. And, the only silver in the town were the coins used to buy supplies or change hands at all-night poker games while paying for an abundance of booze.

One bitter cold night during a blinding snow storm, a not-so-young man on a mangy old mule drifted slowly into Silver City looking for a way to get out of the cold. He could have been cast as a drifter in a western movie with his unshaven and downtrodden appearance. He stopped in front of the only lighted building on the edge of town — the Blacksmith's shop. He carefully slid off his ride and walked into the building.

"Howdy," he said to the young man pounding a piece of metal that was glowing from the heat of the fire next to him, "my name is Jake." The young man nodded back and said, "Tom here," as he continued working. There was an empty stable in the back of the shop and the stranger asked if he could bring his mule in out of the cold. The blacksmith gestured his approval.

That night was the beginning of a simple and wary connection between Jake, the crusty old man and Tom, the intense young blacksmith. Tom knew that drifters usually had pasts that were better left hidden and Jake was cautious not to undo his welcome by prying into Tom's history.

Jake was too proud to admit he was almost penniless, so for the next week, he helped around the place in exchange for a spot in the stable for himself and his mule. However, Jake needed cash for food and supplies, and Tom could only offer the bare bones lodging in the stable.

There was not much opportunity for work in Silver City, so Jake felt lucky to get a bartending job at the local saloon that included a one-room apartment upstairs. He had no intention on staying long.

However, his old mule took a turn for the worse and he had to bury him a few weeks after getting into town, which left him without transportation. Sticking pretty much to himself, Jake's only connection to society seemed to be the hours spent pouring drinks and listening to stories told by those who frequented the bar.

A few years passed, then one night Tom came into the saloon. He seldom drank, but Jake understood why the young man would want a drink after hearing earlier that day that Tom's friend had been working in one of the old gold mines when it collapsed and buried him alive. Tom sat for several hours at the end of the bar without saying a word. After several drinks, Tom slowly looked up from his almost empty glass and cleared his throat. "Why in the world are you still here in Silver City?" he asked. Jake was surprised at the question. Actually he was surprised that Tom even wanted to talk. Even though they lived in the same town, they rarely spoke.

Jake walked over to Tom tossing his bar rag on top of the bar and resting his elbow on the polished wood surface while he thought of his answer. "*More than one winter has found me working in a Silver City dive that beckons to the thirsty with a classic neon sign of a cactus in the foreground and a horseman drifting alone into the distance.* This has become my life, I'm too old and too tired to move on. You might say the neon sign lights my way."

A POEM BY DELL BLACKMAN

How Can This Be

Some say ...
they fell in love
or,
out of love
Like taking a dip
in a pond
along the trail
I ask ...
how can this be
Perhaps, they were
only splashing
on the surface
Or, floating
on a reflection
that was deeper
than
they could see.

Prompt #9

Mysterious And Wondrous Ways In Which Libraries And Animals Enrich Humanity

I never thought I was someone who had to have pets, but in looking back, I realize I have always had pets. Quite a few of them, actually. There was Puddy, our first cat when I was a child and Cheddar Cheese, our first dog. We also had a small green turtle which didn't survive very long.

During my teenage years I had two cats — one caramel colored Persian named Nathan and a chocolate Burmese cat aptly called Bernie. My parents had a small poodle named Killer — it was the only name he would respond to! They had tried to call him Charlie, but to no avail.

Later, when I got married, the real zoo began. We had Little Boots, a long haired butterscotch-and-white cat, Mittens, a tiger cat with six toes, Cujo, my son's ferret, Chilio the chinchilla, two Chow Chow's — Dejah and Kody, two Samoyed's, Toby and Sheba, two small doves, three turtles, a large 55-gallon fish tank and a couple of other cats and kittens that belonged to my two daughters. That's a lot of pets!

Last but not least was Kuvasz, a pure white long haired dog from Tibet. Kuvasz was special. She was a gentle dog with a deeply loving, aware and spiritual nature. Of all of them, I miss Kuvasz and Mittens the most. They were the ones that left a deep hole in my heart when they were gone; an obvious vacancy of love.

I've often thought I should write a story about the things that have enriched my life — animals being one of those things and books being the other. I have always loved libraries, books and bookstores. I loved it when Barnes n' Noble and Borders Books opened with their cozy chairs and cafés within. Libraries too would have their quiet spaces where you could sit and read in the silence. There is something about being surrounded by books that heals the soul. It was wonderful that our small writing group began on the second floor of Dudley's Bookshop Café in downtown Bend, Oregon. I believe it was being surrounded by a plethora of bookshelves filled with all manner of subjects that allowed my dormant imagination to come alive again. Yes, books excite me! All that information and imagination — authors putting forth their ideas, biographies and histories.

Ah, the *mysterious and wondrous ways in which libraries and animals enrich humanity!*

CHARLES SCAMAHORN

I stood in awe in front of the big desk in one of the biggest library reading rooms in the United States. The University of California Berkeley Doe Library is enormous, and the designers back in 1911 spared no expense in making it a clarion call to scholars all over the world that this is where they should spend their academic lives.

Making my astonishment and awe deeper and even more humbling was the young woman behind the counter. She was so beautiful it made my toes tingle, and when she spoke her obvious intelligence let me know instantly I was in the right place. She was so interested in helping me get what I wanted that I soon forgot my own anxieties and followed her over to the exact book I was searching for. That book was a common book a few years before in some places, but now it was rare and only available in a research library. Probably the Library of Congress would have it, but that was several thousand miles away. I came back to that shelf of books several times and a week later I asked that librarian if she would have a coffee with me at the local coffee shop. She said she couldn't. She was a graduate student at the UC library school and next week was final exams, and she didn't have time.

A few days later I was running through campus, coming back from the top of Grizzly Peak where I ran to from my home twice a week. It was a nine-mile run with 1,662 feet of elevation gain, and I had run that route about 500 times. I was in great physical shape and I was even running marathon races occasionally. That's when it happened.

She was sitting on a park bench as I ran by on my way home, more or less at my top speed — I always pushed myself when running — and after some fifty steps more, I thought I should go back and ask her if she would have coffee with me after she had finished her finals. As it happened she was going to give a verbal presentation in about ten minutes, and she was obviously terrified. Speaking before an audience is one of the most stressful things there is for most people, and speaking before your professors for your final exam has got to be at the top of the anxiety scale.

There she was all anxiety ridden and studying her notes, and there I was all sweaty and panty from having run to the top of Grizzly Peak. It was a strange situation. Yes. Tomorrow at noon. That was how I met Debbie thirty-one years before. Yes, libraries have been mysterious places for me and my animal nature, and one of the *mysterious and wondrous ways in which libraries and animals enrich humanity.*

HARRIETTE HOOVER GREEN

This tale is translated into the common language of the land by the most renowned linguists in the world. The origin of the people who left these documents is assumed to be from this planet, Earth. The translation is a rough meaning; some guesses have been used. The writings were found in a time capsule in Iceland in the year 2045. In addition to all the books and moving pictures depicting these people, is a large container of seeds with planting instructions, "For whomsoever finds them." These are pure seeds with no contamination from GM (genetically modified) seeds.

The information in the documents is quite surprising and a little befuddling. See what you think.

These people are of a different race from us. They do not seem to be Krenaken's, judging by their design and behavior. They are tall and without body hair. They are animal in nature and stupid of intellect, judging by their animalistic, aggressive behaviors noted in the pictures. They are not unlearned, judging by the volumes of books sitting on shelving found stored in huge buildings, called libraries — the seats of great knowledge that are located throughout the land. These people have access to great knowledge, but demonstrate no sense. Everything we've found from inside the building indicates they did not learn from their own history. In the big buildings holding the books, are also moving pictures of the people talking in their strange tongue and doing the oddest things imaginable for us Krenaken's, like crashing vehicles into each other in what looks like a great arena. There are several pictures of events of two people punching or kicking, or wrestling with each other or riding beasts that are bucking and kicking to get the human off. These events all seem to be for fun, yet there is such sadness about them. The people seem to be very unhappy even though many of the moving pictures are of humans laughing joyless laughs. There are no pictures of the beings kissing or rubbing noses. They are a strange people.

By viewing the moving pictures we see great abundance. Huge buildings, moving vehicles, play lands with many moving structures where the people are laughing and seem to be having fun. The people have very functional attire, places to live and ability to eat abundantly. But, where is the soul in their culture? Look at the results of their abundance! Look at their hatred against each other, and see the results of their warring! Vast cities have been left in ruins with no people.

It must be noted for our people to stay away from this place. Avoid this planet completely. If for any reason you need to land there, never cross the Bering Strait, stay south and clear of the sickness that is there. Take heed whoever reads this text, this is a place of sickness of the most horrid kind. It is a sickness of the mind, heart and soul.

We must be sure that our people do not become tainted with it, whatever this sickness is. This scouting team will learn as much as we can about the sickness and note it in our journal for future people's to read. We will teleport the information to our people before we return home. It is a vile thing that has happened here.

There are two things of note, we see no pets. The only animals noted are the kind bred for food. Also of note is that there are very few children in the pictures. Both the children and the animals are missing. We have uncovered no explanation for the destruction to some of the cities, like the one called Detroit. The pictures have grown people and old people, but the youngest children are about 10 years old by our estimate. It must have been a plague that killed the animals and the young. No race can survive without children and pets. Our children and pets are what brings joy to one's heart. This is a very sad discovery. We are so very sorry for these people. We will continue to search for clues before we depart, but we don't want to stay too long in case there is contamination.

Journal entry: 400,888.99: The buildings in the north around Washington, D.C. are all empty. There are no signs of people anywhere, just the empty buildings and vehicles. As we traveled south we saw people. One city was bustling but the people seemed joyless. The journal stops at this entry.

It is a mystery we must understand. Our peoples are at risk if we do not. There is an entry by the people from China to find out why the communication satellite was not working and why no one has responded to their calls and attempts to communicate for the last several days. They were rebuffed by Washington, France, Germany, Italy, England. No one would shed light on why the satellite was not working and no one seemed to care. Everyone was acting very strangely. Is everyone ill with this sickness?

Our team leader Kocao suggests we move on now and get back home. We will make contact with you tomorrow night as planned, to confirm we will be teleporting home at 2300 hours. The scientist will continue reviewing the last of the moving pictures. There is a strange rhythm throughout the films, but the rhythm changes as the dates move forward. Things seemed fine until the beginning of 2017 when Trump took the presidential office. That is when the rhythm began to rev up. There is increasing anger and hostility throughout the land. It feels like a tug of war and there is a pervasive feeling of hopelessness.

One film shows the leader of North Korea firing missiles and ignoring demands by the western countries to stop. This is when a rocket is launched at these people and all goes black. That is the last piece of film with the most recent date.

Wait! The team is running with a newly found container. The pictures we are now viewing show the leader of North Korea, Kim Jong-un with a little puppy. He is holding the puppy close to his chest. He then nuzzles the puppy to his face. He kisses the puppy and rubs noses. He speaks to the camera and bows, again and again and again as he holds the puppy close to his heart. The broadcaster speaks in Korean, but the subtitles are in the common language of the land. He thanked the great western countries for the gift. He is proud to accept the gift. He promises to keep him safe from the great illness and offers peace to all lands!

Kim Jong-un explains he has been studying the western ways by reading in his country's library's the meaning of LOVE for one's self by loving one's family and nation, including animals. He has sent one last rocket that will dispense the potion to awaken the sleeping children and pets. He asks that we all live in peace.

The great mystery has been solved! We can leave knowing all is well in this part of the Universe. We will title our log, *Mysterious and wondrous ways in which libraries and animals enrich humanity!* Thank the Great Source.

KEVIN O'GRADY

The old man was oblivious to the dog cocking his leg against his pants until the warm yellow liquid soaked into his woolen sock.

"Jeepers, creepers!" he mumbled in a polite, contained kind of way, aware that he was in the company of an 11-year-old who loved dogs. His usual unbridled response would probably have him arrested where he stood right outside the public library.

"Let's go inside and get cleaned up," he said, reaching down for his granddaughters cold hand. They had been inseparable since she was born. She had heard more than once her grandfathers eloquence when he thought she wasn't around and he was free to let his anger rip. All his life he was angry about everything. He grew up in the great depression with little food and no money. He got part-time work after the war in a coal mine, which he didn't like, and after 76 years of life he still found himself in the same coal mining town where he began work over 60 years ago.

Since his granddaughter had been born, things had been improving. He felt his life was more tolerable, even worth living. The incident with the dog even reminded him of how lucky he was to still be alive after the Search and Rescue dogs searched him out from under piles of dirt and coal-dust in the great coal mine collapse of 1947. But he still felt ungrateful, and many times wished that he had died that day.

"I must learn to love dogs", he mumbled to himself, as they entered under the grey granite facade of the towns only library. Its old fashioned architecture and dark outer appearance belied the rich bright interior.

"That must be how I look", he muttered to himself. "I'm old and gray, but I'm full of knowledge and wisdom on the inside."

His egotistical reverie was interrupted by what he saw as he entered through the big oak doors. The library was full of dogs! There was a huge banner hanging from the ceiling saying, *National Guide Dog Day*. Old and young alike, hundreds of blind people lined up and down the isles, all oblivious to the huge *Quiet Please* signs that hung on the bookcases in every aisle. They chattered and laughed and joked as if they were in the local bar on a Saturday night.

"Come, granddad. Can I pet the dogs?"

Such innocence, he thought. "Of course, dear, but make sure to ask permission first." The old man spotted the men's room across the great hall. "Wait here," he instructed the child, "I'll be right back when I get cleaned up." Just then, a guide dog, smelling the scent of a rival alpha male on his trouser leg stood almost innocently by his side, and was about to lift his leg when the 11-year-old squealed, "Watch out granddad. Run!"

The old man tripped in fright, and found himself lying at the feet of the Chairman of the Joint Library Committee for the Blind, his black Labrador licking his face.

"What have we here?" the Chairman asked, poking his white stick into the old man's stomach.

"It's me, Jerry Collins," he said.

"Jerry Collins from the 14th Infantry Division?"

"Yes, that's me."

"Jerry Collins who we rescued from the coal mine in 1947?"

"Yes, that's me!" said the old man, looking up slowly at his rescuers from all those years ago. "My God," he muttered, "this is one of those *mysterious and wondrous ways in which libraries and animals enrich humanity.*"

Marion was just five years old when she decided that one day she wanted to be a Librarian. When asked what she wanted to be when she grew up, Marion had a ready answer.

Perhaps it was because her mother brought her to the library every week to pick out a few special books that they brought home and read together. Or, maybe it was her love for story hour on Thursday afternoons, because the story lady made every book she read come alive in Marion's imagination.

Now, sixty years later, Marion was about to retire as the Head Librarian of the very place she had loved all her life. She was well-known for her dedication to not only the library, but to the town's people; having never married, the children and other patrons of the library had become her family.

There had been talk about closing the library since most folks used their computers to gain access to needed information, or read books on their eBook Readers. Nothing was the same.

More recently, the library had become a place of refuge from bad weather for some of the folks who lived on the street; and fewer and fewer groups used the all-purpose room for meetings. Marion was actually relieved in some ways that it was time to retire.

The local paper ran a nice story about Marion and the library as a farewell to her years of service. She knew so many people in town that during her final week at the library, many current and former patrons stopped by to wish her well, and in many cases, thank her for her help throughout the years.

That final day, the mayor asked Marion if he could stop by in the afternoon to meet with her briefly. Always gracious, she asked him to come by just before closing time. Later that day, she was going through a small stack of papers in her office when she heard some commotion. She went to investigate only to find the Mayor and about fifty other townspeople gathered in the reception area.

The local bakery had supplied a huge sheet cake, and some of the children were holding brightly colored balloons. Marion felt a lump forming in her throat. It was so touching to have such a special celebration just for her. The Mayor shared a few stories related to "Marion the Librarian" and all she had done for so many.

Then, he told his own story of how he hid out in the library one day to avoid having to go to school when he was ten years old. When Marion discovered him sitting in a dark corner at the end of a long row of bookcases, she sat down on the floor next to him and asked him why he was there. She was so kind and didn't give him a bad time for skipping school, so he finally told her he just didn't like school. In her gentle way, she asked him what he wanted to be when he grew up. He told her that he was not real sure, but thought about being a veterinarian because he loved animals.

"How do you plan to become a veterinarian if you don't finish school?" she asked.

He didn't have an answer.

Marion stood up and walked over to the biography section and pulled a book off the shelf. "You might want to read this before you decide to skip school again," she said, handing it to him. "It is about a boy who loved animals and wanted to help them when they were sick or when they got hurt. He studied hard and became a veterinarian who helped many animals during his career. Eventually, he decided to go into politics, and actually became the mayor of the town he loved so much."

The Mayor was wiping a tear as he told the story to the crowd. "That day was a turning point for me," he explained. "And I owe it all to Marion the Librarian. I guess you might say that there are *mysterious and wondrous ways in which libraries and animals enrich humanity.* Both have certainly enriched mine."

Speak to me Softly

Speak to me softly
in the shadow of my soul
Tell me the ways of wisdom
and all that I should know
If by chance...
love flickers into a flame
May it burn away the fear
so I'll never be the same.

Prompt #10

One Way Or The Other,

That Gives

Poetry Its

Musical Qualities

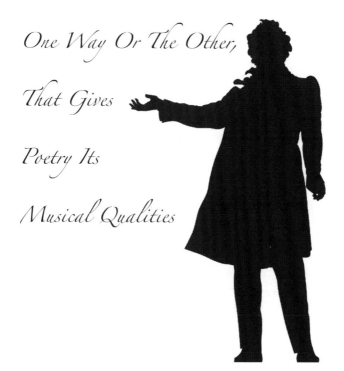

AINGEAL ROSE O'GRADY

It was in the Seventh Heaven where Maribel had resided since she emerged as a spark of light. She came out as the 32nd tone on the musical scale and she emitted a beautiful yellow golden aura mixed with effervescent sparks of crystal light. She was obviously female in her vibration and she wouldn't have had it any other way.

The Seventh Heaven was a radiant place. The atmosphere undulated with a multitude of frequencies and colors that shifted and changed moment by moment. Being embedded in music and color daily was what Maribel knew as life. Other beings in the Seventh Heaven spent their time creating poetry. One couldn't tell if the colors and musical notes in this place were natural to this level or if it was the poetry created daily that took its form as music and color. It was obvious that *one way or the other, that gives poetry is musical qualities.*

Maribel didn't spend her time contemplating and creating poetry. She was much too dynamic for that!

Being the 32nd note on the musical scale, she wanted *effects*. She wanted to cause profound changes, jar reality into expressions it had never before demonstrated.

So, it came as no surprise that she would want to explore beyond or below the Seventh Heaven. All of it was a smorgasbord of wonder to Maribel! But how could she leaves this place? Where was the doorway out? Above, below, or sideways? No one that she knew that resided here had ever left or ventured out beyond the Seventh Heaven boundaries, not even for a day.

So, her search began. She decided that whichever doorway she found first, that would be the one she'd take. First, she set herself down in the Temple of Frequencies that drew in light and sound from all directions and pooled them into the center. One could immerse themselves in this pool and be rejuvenated or simply travel on the various frequencies in their consciousness.

Maribel's purpose this day was to invite in the frequencies and waves that would, one way or another, open her first doorway to another Heaven. She immersed herself in the pool. Waves of disturbance filled her being. The waves were chaotic, sharp and irritating. Maribel was suddenly taken down a dark hole in the center of the pool. There was nothing she could do. The force of it pulled her deeper and deeper downward and the hole was becoming more and more narrow, exerting a suffocating pressure on her.

She was spiraling out of control and then suddenly, as quickly as the hole had sucked her in, it spat her out and she landed with a thud on a cold and dark surface.

Maribel lay there for what seemed like hours trying to orient herself. She was dizzy and found it hard to get her bearings. On the one hand, she was delighted to have arrived somewhere new and on the other hand, she hadn't quite expected the coldness and darkness of this place. It was not filled with the colors that permeated the Seventh Heaven, nor was there any music to be heard. No one was creating beautiful poetry. In fact she saw no one at all.

Maribel stood up, shook herself off and began her exploration. The landscape was unusual. She couldn't float here, getting from one place to the other took effort. She had to stop often to catch her breath. There were hills and valleys here, rocky spots and then smooth spots. And the darkness was everywhere. And the coldness stayed.

After some hours Maribel noticed a faint lightening of the sky overhead. An excitement and curiosity came over her. She jumped up and watched the light intently. First, it came slowly, softly and then it burst forth with a fury of fire. It was something she had never seen before. It was a sun being newly born! And although she didn't know it, *she* had been the cause. After all, she was the 32nd note on the musical scale, the note of pure love!

It was a stormy morning here in Bend, Oregon. Most of the snow had melted away that was exposed in our open fields, but where the snowplows had piled it along the sides of the roads, there were still four-foot-high berms. I had driven to the Unitarian Church an hour early planning to attend a pre-church meditation group, but during the drive over it started snowing again and was snowing heavily when I arrived for the meditation.

By the time I parked, the snow was covering the ground an inch deep and accumulating fast.

The regular services weren't scheduled to begin for an hour, so rather than go to the quiet fireside room and meditate, I decided to shovel snow to clear the paths for the oncoming congregation members. I had done this simple work several times at various places during this week of record snowfall with the intent of developing more mature habits.

My previously posted idea is that when one is feeling good and has some psychic energy they should look around and intentionally choose to do the most mature thing that needs doing.

Shoveling snow may not sound like a mature activity, after all a child can do it, but when one of the great sages of ancient times was asked what he did now that he had achieved enlightenment, he replied, "I chop wood and carry water." His disciple asked him how that differed from before he became enlightened. How did it differ from when he was a youth being forced by his parents to chop wood and carry water?

"It's no different. No different in the physical activity. The difference is in the mental and spiritual activity. As a child I felt rebellious and angry at having to do such stupid things as chop wood and carry water, but now, as what you call an enlightened sage, I feel a satisfying rush that permeates my whole being for the opportunity to be of service to my fellow human beings and to my animal friends and to my plant friends, too." *One way or another that gives poetry its musical qualities.*

Some lyrically inclined people would call this attitude toward those simple acts a form of poetry. It gives structure to an otherwise dumb physical reality. It gives meaning to the results that come from the uses of the water and from the uses of the chopped wood. This attitude generates the most beautiful music that exists in our world.

These simple physical acts that seem so lacking in spiritual meaning ultimately give everything the essentials of life and permit living beings — people, animals, and plants too — to thrive. What could be more poetic? What could be more musical? The rhythmic sound of chopping wood is poetry and it's the finest music that can be made because it is the sound of life being brought into a higher state of being.

Chop, chop—carry, carry—shovel, shovel, shovel.

HARRIETTE HOOVER GREEN

My great-grandmother was a colorful woman, all four foot nine inches of her, which didn't seem so small to an 8 year old girl. The fact that her husband, my great-grandfather, was all of five foot two made it seem normal. There was nothing about this pair that was normal or average at all. They may have been slight in stature but neither was slight of spirit!

We all called them Momo and Dado. having been named by my mother, their first grandchild. She set the name and it stuck for us all. Mom was the first of that generation, named after her grandmother, Momo, and I the first of my generation, named after both my mother and her mother, Margaret.

As the story goes, mom called her *Momo, Oh Mom,* or *Mom oh!* Of course, it followed that grandfather would be *Dad oh!* The point being they were special, recognized very early on by mom and all who followed her. You could call Momo feisty and you would be right; I thought of her as clever.

There was never a challenge she couldn't meet or

solve or *conquer* as she would say, especially in those times when women were not thought to be equal to men, which galled her to her core. I may have assimilated those thoughts and feelings from the air surrounding her mighty little body.

An example of my Momo was the time I was staying with them on their farm in Indiana for two weeks; just them and me. I was eight years old, it was 1949. It did seem like I had gone to Mars or some different world from my home in Michigan. Everything in Momos house was different. I know now it was old fashioned, old like them.

Their refrigerator was an ice box. Yep, a box with a large block of ice, delivered weekly on an ice truck, all the way up the long, winding driveway from the highway to the back door. It was brought in from the ice truck by a man with a pair of huge ice tongs. All very fascinating. He would place it in the ice box on the bottom, after he removed whatever had not melted into the tray below. That is how farm folks lived without electricity in those days.

Their little farm house was at the top of a huge hill. Before the well was dug, out their back door, Dado used to carry one to two buckets of water up the hill once or twice a day, as needed for laundry or bathing. In the winter they would melt snow. When he could no longer carry the water by hand, he would take their Model T down the hill for water. They were of hardy stock, she from England and he from Ireland, still sporting a bit of the brogue.

My mom told me a story about her grandmum from when she was young. She would visit her grandparents and when she became bored, she would say, "Momo, Momo, what can I do?" And in response, Momo would say, "Margaret June, what should you do, pee in your shoe." At that they would both laugh. Momo was full of sayings.

It won't rain if the sun is shining.

An apple a day keeps the doctor away.

A bird in your hand is worth two in the bush.

One way or the other, that gives poetry is musical qualities.

They would then play *I Spy*. Momo was full of ideas for games. Momo was alway an optimist and Dado more of a pessimist, but they were a perfect couple.

I slept in an old fashioned Murphy bed, set in their dining room. They would pull on a handle and open it for me to sleep and in the morning they would close it into itself and all you would see was a tall piece of furniture allowing for more space in the room, since all the rooms were pretty small. It had a feathered mattress that was so soft, warm and cozy. I slept soundly even with all the outdoor sounds, like wolves howling and owls hooting.

Dado had a spittoon made out of brass, and full of dark brown tobacco spit. He could spit that juice from across the room, making his mark almost every time. Granted it wasn't a very big room, but it still was impressive. Momo must have always had an ear open for the sound of the ping, for if she heard the spit and not the ping, she would call out from wherever she was, "Ollie, you clean that up!" He would wink with his twinkly eyes and smile and call out "Now Maggie, you know I will," without moving a muscle. He would whisper to me, "She knows I won't 'cos she will always do it herself, for I never do it good enough for her." They seemed to play games with each other all day long, each getting comfort from knowing each other so well and so long.

I had a hard time adjusting to some of the ways on the farm, especially on the first visit when I was only eight. I especially didn't like the outhouse (outdoor toilet with no running water and no toilet seat, just a hole)! I will say, the fact that it was a three-holer with big, medium and small holes helped me feel better about the whole idea. Momo tried to reason with me when I refused to use it. I was sure something like a big snake would jump up and bite my behind.

Nothing ever bit me or Dado in all those years, and no one ever fell in. Then Dado would chime in saying, "Well, except Uncle Willie, he hasn't been seen since visiting the outhouse!" They would both chuckle and smile. I used the bedpan, which I had to empty myself. I waited until I could wait no more. Yuck! That changed my tune!

And there was this fancy looking telephone on the wall with a crank. If you wanted to make a call you would wind it up with the crank and the operator would come on and say, "Number please." Sometimes someone else was on the line talking when you picked up the receiver off the hook. They would say, "We are on the line, off in a minute." If Momo was talking and someone would interrupt, she might get snippy, depending on who it was. She would say, "Off in a minute, don't get your shorts in a wad!"

Another feature at the farm were the chickens. They wandered everywhere, *buck, buck, buck* with their heads bobbing up and down as they scratched for food. I was always amazed by how they would go from fluffy little yellow chicks to big multiple colors and from sweet to mean. They didn't like it when I tried to collect their eggs.

Besides the toilet, my biggest dilemma was the water. It tasted terrible, "From the minerals," Momo said, but that wasn't the worst part — it was the fact that frogs swam in the top of the well. I absolutely refused to drink the water. Momo explained how the system worked. I would just shake my head, *No!* Then she said, "One way or another you'll drink water! Ollie, let's chip some ice off the block and let it melt for our little Joanna to drink water."

I was 13 the last time I stayed at the farm. When I left I knew I wouldn't ever see either of them again. Our goodbye was pretty formal, but I felt the love they had for me and for each other every day by trying to accommodate my needs.

Goodbye Momo, Goodbye Dado, I love you. That is the end of the story of the farm and the story of Momo and Dado, but I see them now and again at night in the dark skies as the stars sparkle, reminding me of their twinkling eyes.

KEVIN O'GRADY

Clara sat at the piano and turned to the window to gaze across the rooftops of her Santa Clara home. *Clara from Santa Clara*, she thought. *My dear mother died before she could tell me if she named me after the city, but now it's time to reread her letter to me.*

Clara shifted her position on the piano stool and slowly opened the gray manila envelope that simply said, "From Clara to Clara." She had read it a thousand times, but something told her this time it would be different. The aching in her heart for a deeper meaning to her life, for real love, had been growing since she turned 44, and her recent divorce had left her vacant and alone.

"My dearest, beautiful Clara," the letter began, "you will be without me when you read this, but you will not be alone."

Then it took on a poetic form, reminding her of her schooldays learning the Sonnets of Shakespeare.

* * *

"I will not be here to see your beautiful face
or on your cheek to plant a kiss
or even somewhere to call you on the phone
but here I am at heavens gate
as though it always was my fate
to deliver you into earths domain
and Santa Clara will sing its own refrain
— for you"

"That's it!" she exclaimed. "She gave me the gift of music. And now I must use that gift to bring happiness. Her lines were poetry, and I never saw it. She used the magic of words to turn sound into music. *One way or the other, that gives poetry its musical qualities*."

Clara turned to the piano and started playing. She played as if her mother sat beside her — a duet in Clara Major. Her fingers slipped across the keys like lace on naked skin. She soared into the heights of ecstasy as her joy wrapped her heart in love, and she burst into song with words that came from across the aeons of time.

"I am with you Clara, Clara
I am not one but two
I am like Gone With The Wind at Tara
I am so in love with you."

* * *

The conductor waved his wand and the orchestra began. First violins, then tubas, then trumpets, then big bass drums. The Santa Clara choir brought the annual Philharmonic Music Awards ceremony to a magical close as Clara took center stage. As she approached the microphone for her acceptance speech, she felt for her mothers manilla envelope in her pocket and spoke just seven words.

"From Clara, To Clara. I love you!"

The professor stood before the class. He was crowned with wild and wiry grey hair that looked as if he had just dragged himself out of bed. Trying not to be too judgmental, Jenny could not help but wonder what had happened to the academic world since she had been a young college student. She had expected a professor to look a bit more polished.

Jenny sat in the front row for her comeback to college. After raising her children and losing her husband to a heart attack, this was her first attempt to return to school in over thirty years. Her thoughts crept through her head, crowding out the professor's words. Maybe she waited too long to fulfill her dream of getting a teaching degree; she was starting to have second thoughts about this decision. Sadly, she wondered if she was just an old fool. Sadness spread throughout her being, and the awareness of her mood swing was interrupted by the presence of a tall form standing in front of her as she caught the end of the professor's comment, "*One way or the other, that gives poetry its musical qualities."*

Jenny avoided looking up at the teacher. What in the world was he talking about? Hopefully he was looking over her head at the rest of the class and not directly at her.

In the back of the room one of the students was asking a question, but all Jenny heard was a pair of scruffy, sock-less shoes walking over to the other side of the room as her gaze continued downward. What happened to her? She was never one to be judgmental, and yet she was nitpicking everything about this experience. She had never felt so out of place.

Jenny mused over the question, "What gives poetry its musical qualities?" She wondered what was so musical about poetry. She was feeling a little sick to her stomach at the thought of poetry in general. She could still remember her first love as he handed her a poem he had written for her on the back of an old envelope many years ago. She read the poem and watched him walk out of her life as she tightly clenched the poem into a crumpled ball in her hand.

Even all these years later, Jenny remembered the words as if they were written on the blackboard in front of her:

Run, flee, walk softly from me.
We've touched each other's lives at an awkward moment.
Run, flee, walk softly from me, but step lightly my love,
for you walk upon my heart.

* * *

Wow! That poem brought back a flood of memories. All these years later the memory tugged at her heart, but it did not sound a bit musical! That poem changed her life. She sunk into a deep depression and soon afterwards dropped out of school, returning to her hometown to work in her parent's bakery. Six months later she met her future husband and never thought of that poem until now.

Jenny thought about the life she had lived and felt grateful. It had taken her a few years after she lost her husband to face being without him, but thankfully she was left with some financial comfort and her grown children were settled in their lives. She loved being a grandmother, taking long walks and planning a yearly excursion with two of her best friends. But she couldn't help but wonder if there might be something more for her to do.

More than once over the years, she had thought about getting a college degree. But was it really her dream or an old regret she had held onto? She was brought up by parents who had preached the importance of a college degree as if there should be no other goal in life. On the other hand, not having a degree sometimes gave her an excuse to not reach for something bolder or brighter or bigger.

Jenny wondered why she was focused on her professor's appearance rather than what she was there to learn.

Was this English class going to bring her joy? Was she wanting something more? Was she returning to school to appease her parent's wishes from so long ago, or was she wanting this for her own fulfillment? Without realizing it, Jenny stood up, books in hand, and walked out of the classroom. Perhaps there was something more to discover than what gave poetry its musical qualities.

A POEM BY DELL BLACKMAN

The Happy Boss

The heart
Passed the mind
In the hall
The other day
Stopping the mind
The heart
Had this to say
Listen we're on
The same team
Don't go crazy
Or, shut down on me
Follow my lead
And ... you will see
How happy
The boss can be.

Prompt #11

She Wanted This Couple To Be Comfortable,

But More Importantly,

She Wanted Them

To Stay Long Enough For

Them To Get All The

Answers They Needed

So Desperately

AINGEAL ROSE O'GRADY

Liz sat up straight in her chair. She fumbled with her skirt, smoothing out the wrinkles that had gathered from the five-hour long drive to Salisburg. She had been looking forward to this day for months, and had been studying daily for the past year. She didn't want to fail. In fact, she wanted to pass with flying colors. This had been her childhood dream — one that had gotten waylaid early on in life due to family circumstances beyond her control. Her family had been tossed here and there due to financial difficulties, leaving Liz in a state of high anxiety and low self-esteem. She never felt she knew where she belonged and this journey to Salisburg was the first thing she had ever done that she felt was the right path for her. She was excited and filled with anticipation. She didn't even mind that this exam would last all weekend — it meant that her childhood dream was becoming real. She would finally become an official Muse — someone who would inspire, work magic, and cause others to fulfill their dreams.

This wasn't a fairy tale out of Greek mythology, this was an actual profession right here on planet Earth! Few people knew this — it was considered a *museical* event to even discover this school which was aptly camouflaged as, *The Museical School of the Arts.* Becoming a Muse was definitely an art form and only those who understood the lingo were ever accepted. Liz had passed her initial interview successfully and the exhilaration she felt was a confirmation for her that she hadn't been out of her mind her entire life.

The instructor entered the room and handed out the exam sheets. The exam would determine if one had the unusual gifts required for official Muse training. There were only three others in the room — another woman named Holly and two men, Robert and Barry. The exam was to last three hours the first day and two hours the next with some purposely designed Muse challenges intermingled in the off hours.

Unbeknownst to Liz, the exam on day two was her first job — it was a young couple in their twenties that had just lost their girl child of seven years to a reckless driver swerving his way over the curb and into their front yard, killing their sweet Maeve. They were out of their minds with grief and it would be Liz's job to bring inspiration and new life back into them. She would be introduced to them only as their grief counselor. They would be staying in a comfortable rooming house attached to the school.

Liz had brought them over and shown them their room. *She wanted this couple to be comfortable, but more importantly, she wanted them to stay long enough to get all the answers they needed so desperately.* It seemed to be a daunting task for a new Muse, and evermore so since it was part of her official Muse exam. Liz made sure that the couple's room was next to the budding spring lilac bushes so that the fragrance and perfume of the lilacs would permeate their emotions. There was a library of books just down the hall from their room with couches and overstuffed chairs, inviting those who entered to immerse themselves in knowledge, poetry, novels and humor. Liz had carefully chosen books that uplifted and inspired, those that would transport any reader to a higher place. Part of the grief counseling process for this couple was that they each spend two hours per day in this library. It wasn't a requirement that they pick up a book to read, only that they spend time here daily. Soft music played in the background and glass windows looked out onto vast gardens of blossoming flowers, green grass and fountains.

On the fourth day, Liz brought this young couple out into the garden and left them there. She knew they would become lost, as this was no ordinary garden. This was a Muse's garden, one with unexpected twists and turns designed to confuse the mind. This was for the purpose of jarring the couple out of their grief perceptions so they could open to new experiences.

The couple was left here and soon lost their way, as was the plan. Nightfall was coming upon them, but the soothing temperatures in the garden remained unaffected. They had called for Liz numerous times, but she had not answered them, although she was aware of their calls. It was part of the plan that they stay in the darkness of night, lost to the outside world and in total silence, as part of the healing process. The couple eventually laid down on a soft patch of grass and held each other tightly as they wept, their grief pouring out of their eyes and landing on the blades of grass beneath them. As each tear landed, a new flower blossom appeared, and soon there was a carpet of multicolored buds surrounding them. As their hearts melted they found they were being filled with love and a desire to live life to the fullest. Their entire bodies soon were also filled with the feeling of appreciation and love for life — for *their* lives. For what they could still be and do.

The next morning Liz greeted them in the garden. The path was clear, the day was new, and a warm breakfast was waiting for them. It was a new day and Liz had passed her exam!

CHARLES SCAMAHORN

Charles asked, what is the real question behind the question, "What is it that you need to know and do to help another person be comfortable?" Everyone often says they are seeking happiness and comfort, and many of them go to hear an off-the-cave-wall reply from some guy with long hair pulled into a ponytail, or perhaps left to grow and flow and get horribly tangled, or perhaps wearing some really weird clothes, or perhaps sitting near naked conspicuously situated in the middle of the marketplace, or sometimes living in a barrel, sometimes on a tall column, sometimes standing on a soapbox with a hangman's noose around his neck in Hyde Park in London. All of those gurus are giving us their truths, giving us their ultimate realizations spoken from a place more extreme than a normal person's moment of desperation.

The wild words come from those who not only know they are going to die in the long run, in the abstract distant future, but now. These are the people speaking from the edge of oblivion and they know it's their time to vanish into the void of eternity and for them, it's now. Right *now*!.

Their end will come right at the moment they finish this sentence, perhaps even before they finish it, perhaps this very inst... !

Are these desperate folks at the moment of their death giving us the answers we need for living our daily lives?

And yet, what do they know that is going to be helpful to us, to me? Probably I'm not going to die in this very instant. After all, I'm in good health and statistically, I have maybe ten years to live, and if I act on the advice these desperate people are offering me in their last moments of life, most of my future life is going to be miserable.

If I live every moment for instant gratification all my money will soon be gone and I may soon be living in a barrel being rolled around the town square, or if I satisfy my desire for candy or instant sex or other people's fancy stuff I will soon find myself about to be executed for my moment of self-gratification, for violating someone else's rights and the local laws.

The answers we will probably find most helpful are not the ones spoken by those people living at their extreme moments, but from those people who have found the way to sustain comfortable lives. Thus it appears more reasonable to turn away from those with considerable experience in desperation and seek out those living in tranquility and humor. To talk with mild mannered people in coffee shops about the things they enjoy doing, and not spend much time with the guy hung over a liquor bar, or living in a barrel, or standing on an executioner's box. Oh, yes, we can occasionally listen for a few minutes but then walk away and go to our garden and grow some vegetables and flowers. Or go to a social gathering where people are working on a public works project, building a new highway, or fixing potholes in the old highway. That is, to seek out and find people who are doing something that they enjoy doing for the whole community's good and something that everyone can participate in with helpful actions. That is, they are not fretting about various personal resentments and social injustices, but are treating their fellow human beings better than they treat themselves. They are making everyone's world a better place by their actions. Perhaps those actions need to be motivated by kind thoughts, but it is the external actions that have the meaning. Thoughts and feelings that are not expressed in actions go to the grave if the actions are not completed.

Seeking and getting the pleasure of instant gratification while exerting no personal effort, may work for an instant, but that instant will soon pass and be followed by difficulty and the confusion of trying to bring on another moment of unearned pleasure. Experiencing unearned pleasure is the path to permanent pain.

Judge Judy was in the crowd there in Hyde Park watching the hanging of the infamous predator, Jack the Ripper. *She Wanted This Couple To Be Comfortable, But More Importantly, She Wanted Them To Stay Long Enough For Them To Get All The Answers They Needed So Desperately.* She stood hidden in the crowd amongst some of the victims. She hoped this couple who had been violated would find comfort in whatever Jack had to say from his soapbox on his way to oblivion.

Harriette Hoover Green

The sun was already high in the sky when he opened the door to walk Sedgwick. *Another sparkling day in Central Oregon*, he thought as he leashed his best buddy. What greeted him as he walked onto the front porch was a mess. Bits and pieces of nature's scraps, all over the porch! "What's this?" he exclaimed. It is often windy in Central Oregon, so he assumed the wind blew this debris onto the porch. He stepped over the accumulation and headed out for a brief run, then walk, then run, following his physician's orders. "Don't start out too hard, you'll get sore and over tired and won't want to keep at it," were the words of caution from his orthopod, and friend Dr. Joel Moore who replaced his knee a couple of months earlier. *That is good advice*, he thought to himself, when he realized he was already winded after just three minutes, he noted as he looked at his watch. He slowed to a brisk walk with Sedgwick in the lead. Sedgwick loved the run, but he too had a damaged leg, sustained when hit by a car as a pup.

Sedgwick's owner had not attended his needs, nor were his injuries ever treated. In fact, he was never seen by a veterinarian for anything. His injuries were never treated, no immunizations, he was never neutered. *Poor guy*, was his first thought; he then realized Sedgwick was a lucky guy now, and slowed his pace even more. He loved his dog and companion. Sedgwick was the joy in his life since his wife died and his kids were grown and gone to the four corners of the world.

When they got to the field, they both rested a bit more and he then removed the leash to let Sedgwick run free. He tossed the frisbee and Sedgwick ran to fetch and returned it without hesitation. Another toss and another, when John noticed Sedgwick was limping. "That's enough for now, old boy," at which point the dog flopped down on his side with a 'flump' panting and wagging his tail; he was happy. "Okay guy, we'll head back to the house."

Back at the house they entered through the back, avoiding the mess on the front porch and John started immediately on his computer project from yesterday. "What's this?" He was greeted with a Facebook notification and email from his best friend, Tom.

"Hello John, I hope this post finds you well," wrote Tom. He was coming to Bend and wanted to stop by. *Stop by, nonsense*, John thought. He always stays with me. This was curious. As John read on he discovered why Tom didn't automatically plan to stay with him. He was bringing his fiancée, Frances. He wasn't sure how John would feel about him moving forward with a new woman. Tom knew how much John loved Diane.

Wow, this is big news! John never thought Tom would have another relationship after the horrific death of his wife, Diane occurring in their own home while Tom was on a business trip. Tom was the only suspect, considering no leads and the statistics of women being murdered by their spouse, fiancé or other family member. Tom suffered a hellish year while under scrutiny. He lost everything — his freedom, job, house, furniture, pets, friends, neighbors and reputation as a trusted family attorney. But his family, and the Spiritual Awareness Community of the Cascades stood firmly by his side, knowing he was innocent. *That was five years ago*, he thought to himself. *It will be great seeing Tom again and meeting his fiancée, Frances.* His mind raced through all the things he needed to do; after all he wanted this couple to be comfortable. But more importantly, he wanted them to stay long enough for them to get all the answers they needed so desperately, whether they stayed with him or not.

With that thought he realized that Diane, Tom's murdered wife, would agree that *she wanted this couple to be comfortable, but more importantly, she wanted them to stay long enough for them to get all the answers they needed so desperately*, and for him also.

He sent off a hasty email to Tom stating he was looking forward to their visit and hosting them in his home. He also suggested they plan to stay a few days to enjoy Bend's many things to do and see. "Time to do some catching up old chap," he wrote.

His mind reviewed the days and months of the murder investigation, the horrid depictions of Tom in the newspapers — local, state and national were emotionally crushing for him and all who loved him. He was a very nice, decent, caring and spiritual man who worked to serve the public as the Prosecutor for the State of Oregon. Tom explained he didn't understand how people could even consider him of her murder. The ordeal nearly crushed him. John needed to know that Tom had forgiven him his doubts about his innocence early in the investigation when everything pointed to Tom and everyone was still in shock. John had never quite forgiven himself for doubting his friend. This opportunity gave him a chance to apologize again. He also needed to know whether Tom was able to release and forgive the killer. Living with held hatred in his heart would prevent him from truly living in love, the thing John most wanted for him.

When he returned to his work, he did so with a smile on his lips. *What good news*, he thought and then he shifted his mind back to reviewing the sales for the month to date, planning for the future month and speculating for the year.

The figures were promising; he was in a good mood. His sales were up. He would most definitely make his target goal and bonus. "Great!" he exclaimed as a big sigh whistled out through his teeth.

He pushed away from the computer, reflected for a moment and decided to do some cleaning. He put fresh linens on the guest room bed and put fresh flowers in the room from his garden. He went to the kitchen to look over his supply needs and headed to the market. He worked quickly, mentally noting what he would buy and what he would serve for their meals together. He was certain Tom would prefer to stay with him rather than in a hotel. Tom was always frugal, but no doubt more so now than ever, having lost everything he ever made or owned. *It was tragic*, John thought, yet, he was now free and building a new life.

It was a miracle that the killer had turned himself in to the police. The killer had been a secret admirer of Tom's lovely wife Diane, unbeknownst to Diane or to anyone else. When he approached her at St. Charles Rehab Center where she worked as a physical therapist, and professed his love for her, she laughed, as women do when embarrassed. She was no doubt surprised and shocked with no idea how to handle this situation, and no idea of the degree of his infatuation. *Her laugh doomed her*, John thought sadly. *No!* he thought and stood up straight, shook his head and growled, "Enough of that!"

He turned his mind to his plan for their first supper. Crab canapés, squash soup, garlic bread and a tossed salad with chocolate cake for dessert.

The telephone rang as he was completing his tasks. He was hoping they would be coming soon. It was Tom and they were on their way. While making the chocolate cake he noticed a robin flying by the kitchen window several times. *Hmmm, that is strange*, he thought.

The doorbell rang just as he was finishing setting the table. When he opened the door, there stood Tom, his oldest and dearest friend on this earth and next to him stood his lovely lady, Frances, his fiancée. "What a striking couple you two are," he said, smiling. "Please come in." As they stepped into the house, John's attention shifted to the mess on the porch. He muttered under his breath, "Oh, it's from the robin. It's built a nest right up on that ledge." His company, Tom and Frances, both turned to look where John was looking. "Yes, Tom said, they are building a nest," noting there were two robins, putting bits and pieces into a pile up on the ledge. John smiled and said, "I'm glad I didn't sweep it up, I would want them to be comfortable for their baby robins!" John chuckled as he recalled that very thought he had for his friend and his fiancée.

Pearl moved the plant to the center of the kitchen table, then she moved it twice more before finally deciding to place it on the windowsill of her small apartment. Located on the seafront, her apartment was classed as luxurious, but the limited light from being so far into the northern hemisphere made it seem dingy and unhealthy. It was the most she could afford while at the same time feel she was maintaining her lifestyle as an investigative reporter.

She glanced around the apartment for the thousandth time. She checked the clock, checked the bedroom door, checked the phone. But she kept coming back to check the hastily written note that had been attached to the money plant that was unceremoniously left outside her apartment just three days before.

"Mr. & Mrs. Matlock and our advisor will be here. Stop. Tuesday 3rd. Stop. 3pm. Stop."

She read the punctuation marks like an old-style telegram, each full stop adding to the drama of the intended visit. *She wanted this couple to be comfortable, but more importantly, she wanted them to stay long enough for them to get all the answers they needed so desperately.*

As owner of the only news agency in Anchorage, Matlock believed he knew everyone and everything that happened in the small Alaskan city, but his failure to publish her last report on the strange happenings in the warehouse across from her apartment had her demanding answers at their weekly meeting, and in a shocking response, he fired her for insolence.

She moved the plant from the windowsill and placed it on the kitchen table again, exactly where it was before. She picked up the note again. It really all started happening three days ago. Matlock's note said 3 of them were coming on the 3rd at 3 o'clock.

"Oh, my God!" she exclaimed, looking at the old grandfather clock that was so out of place in her tiny living room. "It's 3 minutes to 3. Get out. Everyone out!"

"Luckily nobody was hurt in the blast," the Fire Chief said. Pearl was standing in the doorway of the warehouse across from her apartment to shelter from the icy northern wind.

Behind her she felt an icy chill coming through the door and it wasn't from the Arctic wind. It was a different kind of chill, the kind that had an evil intent to it as it seethed invisibly behind the warehouse door.

"Do you know what's in this warehouse?" Pearl asked the Fire Chief. She had known him for 15 years and she knew he liked her, but they never moved it forward into any kind of real relationship.

"Yes," he said, "I do, but you have to come to dinner with me to find out."

"Please be serious," she retorted. "I can't believe this. I just survived a murder attempt and you're trying to come on to me!"

"Wait. What? A murder attempt?"

Pearl noticed the sticker on the Fire Chief's helmet. It said, *Sponsored by Matlock*, and then she noticed his eyes flicker green for just a moment.

"Never mind," she said. "I'm only rambling from shock. But do tell me what is behind this door?"

"It's private *Matlock Security* property. This whole area is out of bounds."

Just then her phone rang. All she saw was that it was from area code 333, and then everything went black.

Heading north towards Dead Fish, in the most remote area of Northern Montana, Jim and his new bride, Janet, were looking forward to setting up their 32-foot fifth wheel travel trailer that strained the bolted hitch connected to their old pickup truck, as they drove the winding gravel road through the mountains. They hoped to live in the fifth wheel while building a cabin. To them, this adventure meant freedom from the city life and a chance to, as they put it, *live off grid.*

The young couple met two years earlier at a UFO conference. Their shared interest helped form an instant bond, and they decided to pursue their fascination with UFO's by finding a place to live in an area of the country that had reported a number of sightings. *Dead Fish* seemed to have frequent reported sightings. In fact, it was believed that the town got its name because after every UFO sighting, dead fish floated up on the shore of the lake that bordered the north end of the small town.

Upon their arrival, the couple made a sobering discovery. Dead Fish had only one store that also supplied an old gas tank that had a manual lever for pumping gas. There were three rustic cabins lining the main street; the only street in the town.

No one was in sight. The only sign of life was a few chickens pecking through the weeds around the store front. There was one old goat chewing on a small patch of grass beside one of the cabins.

Jim and Janet parked near the store and walked through the rusty screen door that squeaked loudly, summoning a tiny grey-haired woman from the back room. She was wearing a dirty pair of baggy overalls, topped with a heavy brown flannel shirt that was two sizes too big. She wore rain boots that were covered with dried patches of mud.

"Howdy, what brings you here?", she asked.

"We're headed to a parcel of land just west of here where we plan to settle," answered Jim.

"What in the world would make you want to live in this area; a nice young couple like yourselves?" The woman was scowling at them as she waited for their answer, making Jim and Janet quite uncomfortable.

Should they tell her their plans? No! At this point they just wanted to leave, but curiosity got the best of them as they ignored her question and asked, "How long have you been here?"

"My whole life," she answered reluctantly.

"Do you have family here?"

"Nope. No family. What family I had has either left or died."

"What's the population of Dead Fish," asked Jim.

"Just me and a hired hand who is off fishing more than helping me. We do get visitors when the media or UFO followers show up. That's why the cabins are here. Guess you heard about the UFO's. Is that what brought you here?"

Looking at each other, the couple quietly and hesitantly nodded their answer.

The old woman shook her head as if in disapproval and said, "Of course, what else would bring someone to this God forsaken place? In fact, there is a couple here right now working on an article for some UFO magazine. If you want to stick around, they should be stopping in soon for dinner."

Dinner? Jim and Janet looked at each other. There was a five-stool bar on the far side of the room and only one small lonely table nearby with four chairs. They realized the store also doubled as a bar and restaurant. Other than the mangy old deer head hanging over the bar, and the dusty grocery inventory, there was not much to look at.

Janet couldn't help but chuckle as she wondered what the expiration dates might be on the cans and boxes in the grocery section. They looked like they had been there for years. Just then a middle-aged couple walked in through the squeaky screen door. They were smiling and extended a hand in greeting.

Within minutes they brought up the subject of UFO's and the young couple was fascinated to learn that the couple from the magazine had actually spotted a UFO the night before. Janet was so excited *she wanted the couple to be comfortable, but more importantly, she wanted them to stay long enough to get all the answers they needed so desperately.*

A POEM BY DELL BLACKMAN

Is It Not of Love

Is it not of love
to help one another
Just as goodness
shines a light
in the dark
Need it be
a rendering
of judgement
before a choice
can be made.

Prompt #12

Still There Is The Wonder

Melody rang the doorbell to the old mansion up on the hill. The mansion had been there for centuries and the same family still owned it. Its artful design and elegance was still intact, and it was rumored to have its secrets, as stately homes of this kind often do.

But it was its gardens that made most people talk. They extended for acres and were designed by Joseph and Lily Barrow back in the late 1700s. There were rows of fruit trees, mazes of all manner of flowering bushes, acres of vegetables growing in season and hidden gates with a variety of vines and ivies. Sporadic ponds with lily pads and other greenery made welcome to small varieties of fish, frogs and turtles. It was an eden of delight and the family opened their gardens to visitors from around the world during the summer months.

Melody's visit to the Forsythe mansion this Tuesday was strictly business. She was the president of the local Chamber of Commerce and she made it her business to modernize the small town of Cherry Hill.

The Forsythe family had a major influence on many of the town's policies, they being one of the major money holders in the area. Melody wanted the support of the Forsythe family, and in particular, Mr. John Forsythe. He was the one who had been the thorn in everyone's side whenever there was a decision to be made, stalling on any new policy. He was a young man in his mid 40s, tall with thick, sandy blonde hair and deep blue eyes. His good looks were part of his irresistible charm and his lingering influence.

Melody was determined this day to bend John Forsythe's arm and bring him into the twenty-first century. She would approach him with a polite but stern demeanor. She would not yield to his charismatic babble! She was determined!

The butler politely answered the door and ushered Melody into the large ornate hallway. Her visit was expected and preparations for tea were announced. She was made comfortable in a small sitting room to the right of the library. The room was extremely elegant with lovely soft blue walls and long off-white lace draperies. Filigrees of intricate patterns in gold decorated the walls adding to the welcoming feel of the room. *A good room for negotiations,* Melody thought, *if not to disarm a contrary visitor!*

John Forsythe stood quietly at the entrance to the room examining Melody's demeanor as she waited for him. He always examined his prey before he entered a room, fully sizing up the occupants in silence first. He found Melody to be regal in her nervousness and he liked her proud arrogance. He entered the room with a warm smile rather than his usual emotionless countenance. He extended his hand warmly and the surprise left Melody feeling somewhat disarmed, which annoyed her.

John insisted she leave business matters to later and instead took her on a carriage ride through the vast estate and a lengthy walk through the gardens. *I will not fall for John Forsythe's charms!*, she thought, and so she hadn't.

As John helped her down from the carriage, he looked at her intently and said, "Whatever it is that you want, the answer is *yes*."

"Pardon me sir, but..."

"Not another word," he said. "Send me the details. I'll give you what you need."

Stunned, Melody kept wondering on her way home what had just happened and why. She had been expecting a stark resistance from the handsome Mr. John Forsythe and was ready to put up a fight for her causes, but was instead left speechless and wobbly.

Suffice is it to say that within a year she and John Forsythe were husband and wife and in another year they were a family of three. Forty years later John Forsythe is still saying *yes* to Melody and whenever she looks back, *still there is the wonder.*

What has been bothering me for the last several days is the realization that the Republicans' most popular presidential candidate enjoys hurting people. His most famous statement before becoming a candidate was "You're fired!" It was always said with a pleasurable gusto!

Nowadays, he is famous for saying incredibly vicious things about any and every category of human being imaginable.

So what's your problem? It's just words ... Don't you remember that childhood saying, *Sticks and stones may break my bones but words can never hurt me*? Of course that's a false statement even for a five-year-old; but words spoken by a president, or even a candidate, do hurt people.

Try these words in a cartoon balloon of the president's pointed finger about to be pressed down onto a big red button, "You're fired!"

The fact that the world as we know it would be destroyed by that simple action and those simple words must give every thinking person the shivers.

Step back from the earth a ways in the next cartoon frame, and see it populated with a great number of mushroom clouds, and the words under it, "You're fired!"

I could end this little essay right here because there wouldn't be anyone to read these words. ... But there's still some time.

There was a study done interviewing several convicted murderers in prison, and a scale was constructed of the motives for their murders, called *Stone's Scale of Evil.* At the beginning of the scale were accidental events that led to a conviction, up the scale a bit were self-defense murders, then murders committed to defend another person, followed by revenge for violations of property, then there were murders accidentally committed during the commission of a crime, such as robbery, then deaths resulting from kidnapping where there was extortion for money; and worse murderers were those people who enjoyed killing other people; and, even worse, those who enjoyed torturing people before they killed them. Clearly that is the ugliest and most dangerous type of inhuman being on the face of the earth!

And there's my problem; we now have several top candidates for president of the United States who clearly fall into that most horrible class of human beings ... those who enjoy hurting people. If a person of that character type gets their finger on the big red button, we will reap the biblical whirlwind.

... YOU'RE FIRED ...

Those may be the infamous words written as the
epitaph for our Earth ... our species ... our democratic
system of choosing leaders.

And *still there is the wonder?*

HARRIETTE HOOVER GREEN

This can't be! No! It is not possible! Yet, here is my note to Santa, in my own handwriting. It can't be so. I heard the reindeer hooves on the roof, I know I heard them! She stood there looking incredulously at the list of *Wishes for Santa*!

Meg was 13 years old, starting her Freshman year in High School in the Fall, but she still believed in Santa Claus. All her friends told her that their parents were Santa Claus. She didn't believe her father would buy those gifts for his daughters.

Meg was a very logical girl. Her father was not around much. She was told that her Dad's job was three hours away, so he stayed over and would come home every two to three weeks. When he was home, he rarely interacted with Meg or Alice, four and a half years younger, but did play with the youngest daughter Judy, the baby!

She was his favorite, obviously, Meg had often thought. He played tickle with Judy and if Meg or Alice attempted to join the fun, he would stop the game.

Whenever Judy was naughty, (most of the time Meg thought), he would say, "She's just a baby."

Baby my eye, thought Meg, *she is six years old!* As the eldest, by four and a half years from Alice and five and a half years from Judy, Meg was the second mother to the two younger girls. She would attempt to discipline Judy, and Daddy would scold her and tell Judy it was fine. Meg tried to help her mother who had a real difficult time controlling Judy.

Back to the point. Meg rationalized that her father would not be buying presents for his children. He would not spend his money on anyone, but himself! She was sure about that.

Meg didn't understand why her father was never home like the other fathers in the neighborhood. Or, why they didn't move to the town where he was working, so they could be a family.

She didn't understand his job. Her Mom explained that he was like a traveling salesman. He sold ads for a newspaper, promoted boxing matches and other things she didn't understand, and traveled from place to place with his work. Other fathers worked in the factory, or were laborers.

One dad was a plumber, which sounded really interesting to Meg, who had a curious mind and always wanted to understand how things worked.

Her Mom never had money for anything other than food. Since she was 11 years old Meg earned money babysitting for school supplies and clothes.

There was no money for piano or ballet lessons. There was no money for doctors or dentists. There was no money for anything fun, well, except when her Dad came home after a long spell and he would have Mom drive the girls to the movies and let them see two movies and even gave them money for candy and popcorn. It was sort of like a holiday when he came for a visit, at first.

Everything was nice for a while, then he would get mad about something. If he lost his temper, he would yell at Mom or the kids, storm out, sometimes not coming back until the next visit. As you can see, Meg's Dad did not live with the family. After he left, Mom would cry and cry and be sad for a few days until her happy, sweet nature would return. Then she would dance around, humming or singing and sort of dancing as she worked. Mom was fun and she was pretty, like a delicate flower. She had a big heart and would help anyone in need.

Meg remembered the time a girl got caught in some barbed wire fencing and couldn't get out. The more the girl struggled the more cut up she got. She was just there crying, caught in the fencing when Meg saw her and ran home to tell Mom. Mom dropped what she was doing and the two ran back to the girl. Mom comforted her and calmed her down and eventually got her untangled. They didn't have a car, so they walked the girl back to their house and Mom washed and tended her wounds.

Meg didn't understand how her Mom knew what to do, but she always did. There were many incidents when Meg's Mom was able to save the day, so to speak, in emergency situations with knowledge she really didn't have. It seemed she just knew what to do. Meg was proud of her Mom for those things and also because she was the prettiest Mom in the neighborhood or anywhere Meg had been, and she was nice. Everyone liked her. She also dressed well and always looked pretty even without makeup. She didn't need it.

Back to the Christmas list Meg had composed and tucked under the living room rug, as was the custom in their house. On Christmas morning the girls would sneak down the stairs to see if any of the things on the list had arrived. Meg still loved playing with dolls and paper dolls; dolls were on every Christmas wish list. She played with them even though her Dad said, "You are too old for that now."

She found the list in her mother's robe pocket, proof perfect. She just borrowed her Mom's robe to feel more like a grown up. "If only I hadn't borrowed her robe!" said Meg out loud and started to cry as she thought about her ruined belief in Santa. No more Santa! To Meg, this lie was so big that she asked herself, "If there is no Santa, maybe there's no God!" She noted the similarity between Santa and God. If you are good, good things happened. If you were bad, well, you know what I mean.

As Meg looked back on her childhood from the vantage point of adulthood, she smiled at the memory of that tiny young girl turning into a teenager, but still being very innocent, sweet and naive, loving the fantasy world of make-believe as she played with her dolls and paper dolls creating happy-ever-after stories. She loved to play make-believe. Meg realized the struggle she had with growing up and having to give up her fantasy world to "live in reality," as her Dad said she needed to do.

So, she did give up playing with her dolls and paper dolls exchanging them for going into the forest across from their house and playing with the fairies. She swore she could see and talk to the fairies, and the trees, birds, squirrels and whatever life form she could find. She discovered when she talked to the trees that she knew what they said back to her. Whenever she had a dilemma, she would ask the trees what should she do, and it seemed they sent her the answer into her heart without making any sound.

Sometimes the squirrels would chatter and she would interpret their chatter as the answer to her questions. The forest was magical and more than made up for having to give up her dolls and her belief in Santa. She thought, *It is not that different from learning the Easter Bunny didn't really bring the candy and toys at Easter.* It even helped her like her Dad better knowing he did care and really did buy them presents from Santa.

She realized still there is the wonder in the world that she could trade one way of thinking for another. She even felt a little more grown up, being in on the secret her parents kept. She began thinking that being a parent was hard and began to think her parents were pretty swell. I'm sure they didn't want to live apart, but they needed to sacrifice their wants for a better future.

It was the next summer when they moved to the city where her Dad worked. But, first they rented a house on a lake for the whole summer. It was fun swimming everyday, exploring the woods and looking for the fairies. Her sisters loved the game of looking for fairies. That's the summer that Judy jumped off the dock, but didn't know how to swim. Alice jumped in to save Judy, but she didn't know how to swim either. Meg knew she couldn't swim, couldn't save them herself, so she screamed and yelled for help and several people jumped in and saved them both. She got a lot of kudos for her cool thinking.

At the end of summer they finally packed up to move into their new home. Meg stayed at her grandmother's house the last day because she had her monthly and really didn't feel well. She saw the car pull up and went out onto the porch to greet her family when the most horrible thing happened that could ever happen. Judy ran across the street, not waiting for Mom or Dad to help her. As she ran, she saw a car coming at her and ran diagonally instead of straight. The car hit her. Her little body flew up in the air, came down, and hit the car, falling under the car. Her long hair got caught in the wheel-well and her little body was dragged to the end of the street. She looked like a rag doll. Meg saw it all and couldn't even scream. She ran in the house to get her grandmother shouting, "Call a doctor, call a doctor!" She didn't know how to use the phone or about ambulances or hospitals. Her family never had a telephone.

The next time she saw her sister Judy, she was packed in ice and her head was the size of a pumpkin. She remained in a coma for 30 days. She was famous! Her story was on the news and everyone in the hospital and around town prayed for her. Meg felt really guilty about being angry with Judy for being hard to watch over. She prayed that if she lived, she would not ever get angry with her again. Judy did live, and Meg thought to herself, *still there is the wonder* in the world when someone can be declared dead seven times and yet still survive.

KEVIN O'GRADY

The small deer opened its eyes and the first thing he saw were the adoring eyes of his mother. Although battered, windswept, aging, and sore from scars and constant escapes from mankind, to him she was the most beautiful thing he had ever seen.

She too gazed intently at the delicate bundle of newborn that lay before her. Her thoughts ran to the many adventures that lay in store for her young fawn, then to the many dangers that awaited him in the wild. She thought of the times she explored the vast mountains, through plains and thickets, over hedge and thistle, through forests of pine and oak and beech and willow, and then to the times she lay down with his father in the relative safety of the high gorge.

What future lay in store for him? she wondered, as the sound of a bullet echoed around the lower valley close to where she herself had been born only five short summers before.

The hunters had come too close too many times to her mountainside, a territory marked only by the scent of her soulmate. But one of those bullets had found his heart shortly after the last mating season, and since then, new culling orders were posted in the village Post Office offering bounties for females. His body had been dismembered and left to rot in the dank undergrowth while his antlers were taken as a sporting prize by a man boasting to his sales team.

Where is safe now? she wondered. *Do I take him higher into the peaks, or are we safer in the denseness of the oak forest?*

As her breathing slowed with the gentle, rhythmic breathing of her newborn, she thought she could hear a voice in the distance. It came closer, louder, but she wasn't startled by it. It was the voice of her stag, his voice coming to her across the ethers of time and space.

He said, "Don't be worried my love, my life was not in vain. You and I continue in the new life that lies before you, and like that, we have carried the joy of our being from our ancestors before us. Fear not the greed of some, for the love of life is in all things and all beings."

Just as she was beginning to enjoy his reassurance and the comfort of his words, her heart jumped at the sound of a breaking stick in the undergrowth beside her.

"Don't worry dear one," said the leader of the Wolfpack. "We will lead those hunters away from you. We will lead them towards the river where our friends, the bear-kind, will teach them respect for our ways."

"Oh no, please don't hurt them," she cried. "Our lives all have purpose, and they deserve to live too."

With that, the wolves were gone and so was the reassuring voice of her stag. Her baby fawn stared up at her with its huge brown eyes.

"I want to be just like my dad," he whispered.

"You will be wiser from his courage, my son," she said, as she nurtured him with the love only a mother can give.

As she lay back to rest on the relative safety on her bed of soft green ferns, she heard the voice of her stag again. This time, softer, fainter, more distant.

"I am overjoyed," he said. "I am in the world of life that I did not fully appreciate when I was with you."

The voice grew fainter. In the fast diminishing light of the setting sun, she was sure she heard him say, *And still there is the wonder.*

LINDA KAY

Have you ever wondered why you are here on this planet at this time in your life? This question has puzzled humanity for centuries. Is there such a thing as reincarnation? Is there more to the universe than we'll ever know? Are we here to learn lessons? Why do some struggle so much while others seem to have an easier life? When we die does our soul go to a different plane of existence?

In today's world, one can find most anything on the Internet. Just Google *Secrets of the Universe* and see what comes up. With all the information available on any subject, one would conclude that we can have the answers to all the above questions and many more. On the other hand, with the plethora of information available, it tends to simply overwhelm and confuse most of us.

So, how does one make peace with all these unknowns? No matter how much you research a subject, there always seems to be some difficulty coming up with straightforward and succinct answers. There doesn't seem to be enough time in the day to explore all that we wonder about. And *still there is the wonder.* You might ask yourself, just how much do you really want to know?

Perhaps all anyone can hope for is to find peace with knowing we don't get to know the answers right now; otherwise, we can drive ourselves crazy trying to make sense of it all. Could it be possible to simply trust that there is a higher power overseeing what we are doing here, and that we are living our purpose? And, if you wonder about your purpose, take a look at the highlights in your life, whether it is raising your children, running a business, or giving hope or encouragement to another human being. There are so many different purposes.

There are also those who just never get their life together. If they look closely, they may discover that their purpose is to learn either what it is like to be in the situation they are in, or what it is like to pull themselves out of that situation. Either way, there is a purpose.

Have you heard the expression, *Look within?* We already know the answers we are seeking, however, looking within for those answers is the hardest part. Most people look outside themselves for the answers, or to blame something or someone else for their lot in life. Once we accept the fact that we create the life we are living, we can begin making desired changes.

Another way to look at it is to realize that wherever we go, we take ourselves with us. We are our own common denominator. The answers are not outside ourselves and the Universe is always listening.

Whatever we say to ourselves or others, the Universe is always saying, *Yes*. For example, if you say, *I'll never get a job*, the Universe will say, *Yes, you will never get a job!*

Instead, you might rephrase the above negative statement by saying, *I have now found the right job for me*. Now, the Universe says, *Yes, you have now found the right job*. Which sounds better?

It is amazing to listen, really listen to yourself. What you are constantly saying is what is creating your reality. If you are always saying, *I never have any money*, you will be sure to make that your reality. This may sound too simple. Change your words; change your life. It works!

Instead of trying to figure out huge questions such as, *why are we here?* Why not focus on where you are now in your life and decide to pay more attention to how you created the life you have. Words are what form the life you are living. All you need to do is start reframing what you say to yourself and others.

Often the simplest of suggestions bring the greatest benefit, however, we tend to overlook easy fixes such as reframing what we hear and say. Changing your words changes your experience. Ask, *What would happen if this could really work?*

See Yourself

You have ...
your own voice,
your own calling
to hear and follow
Listen ...
to the humming
of your own vibration
See the style
of your own signature
Stay true ...
to your heart
And, remember ...
all is love
in a place where
no deeper truth exists
So, dive in deep
and see yourself
swimming there.

Prompt #13

The Last Thing She Wanted To Do Was Leave This Place

Helena Montague fixed the bright red ribbon on her summer bonnet. She attached the elegant gold pearl pin that Peter had given her on the right side by the bow. "Now," she said, "that's perfect!" She was on her way to the yearly banquet celebrating local artists and artisans. She was especially exuberant this year as her young daughter, Penny, was one of the entrants. Penny was only 10 but she exhibited a rare artistic talent and Helena was extremely proud of her. All the entrants were to keep their pieces veiled until the banquet officially began. No one knew beforehand what would be revealed. It was designed this way to build the anticipation and assure a sold out crowd.

Helena checked her coat and made her way to her table. She and Penny would be sitting with the McCarthy's tonight, as Peter would be arriving late. Dinner would be first and then the unveiling would commence. The air was festive, people were jovial and friendly. It was a great occasion for the city folk to gather together and celebrate their own.

Finally, the moment arrived. The artisans were to each go and stand by their piece as it would be they themselves who would unveil their piece. Penny was nervous as she was the youngest there and she knew others would be looking to see what one so young could produce.

She wasn't wrong. When it was her turn to unveil her piece, the room fell deathly silent. Not one sound could be heard. Moments seemed like hours for Penny. She didn't know how to read the silence. She couldn't read the expressionless faces. Then the people started to move. Ever so slowly they came closer and closer. They walked around Penny's piece in awkward movements. They all came, every guest and every participant, each examining and gently touching the piece, spellbound by its effect on them. Helena was among them —she too couldn't speak, such was the power that Penny's piece exuded. Gradually, everybody went back to their seats and sat down. And still no one spoke.

Penny too went and sat down, fearing the worst. Did they not like her piece? Are they upset? Had she done something wrong? Should she leave? *The last thing she wanted to do was leave this place*, but should she? Tears of fear began to flow from her eyes. Her cheeks soon had long wet streams that landed like dewdrops on the rose embroidered collar of her dress. She turned and looked at her mother pleadingly. What did it all mean? She needed an answer. Helena put her arms around

Penny, smiled, and held her close to her chest. Her pride could not be contained. Soon she too had tears running down her cheeks, but these were tears of love and praise.

And then, one by one, each person in the room came over to Penny and either shook her hand or hugged her. Whispers of "Congratulations" or "How did you do that?" were the commentaries. All were filled with awe and admiration for the rare gift of Penny Montague.

Little did they know, they had been touched by an Angel.

CHARLES SCAMAHORN

It was the so-called *Summer of Love* in the Haight-Ashbury district of San Francisco, and Abigail was in a state of absolute confusion. She had arrived two months earlier from her home town in remote Central Oregon. That was a small logging town named Bend, and it was only fifty years since the railroad had been built to take out the lumber and bring a modicum of civilization to the local lumberjacks, farmers, and cowboys. It was a beautiful place with mountain views, a fine river, and, if you liked fishing, lots of entertainment. *The last thing she wanted to do was to leave this place.*

The people there in Bend were serious-minded, and their minds were focused on making a living and enjoying their family life. Their social life was comfortable and conservative with the big challenges coming in the form of the annual cooking competitions at the county fair. The life was thought to be as good as it could be, and no one wanted anyone to change their homey lifestyle.

The limit of most folks' ambitions was to make a little more money, add a few more acres plowed on their farm, add a room to their home, perhaps a newer car, but that was it. Life was good the way it was.

Abigail had been named after her grandmother, and her mother had raised Abi to be like her grandmother, and that meant being very conservative but willing to take big risks like her grandmother, who had been a pioneer when she came to Bend in a covered wagon. When Grandma Abigail got to Bend there were fewer than one hundred people, and thus everyone knew everyone and everything about everyone. There was no need for much of what the city folks called law and order, and social pressure kept everyone in line. Even the town drunk. That was the culture that Abi brought to San Francisco and to the *Summer of Love*.

Free drugs, free sex, free rock and roll. That meant cheap pot, cheap sex, and horrible music. Abi didn't like any of it. She didn't participate — she watched, she thought, she rejected it all. Then one day she met Bill. He was a guy from a little town in Idaho, called Homedale. He was so different from the boys she knew back in Bend; he was exciting and had grown up on a farm and knew all about cows and apple trees.

It was only a month into the *Summer of Love* and Abi was pregnant. They decided to move back to Homedale where Bill knew he could get a job. And so they did and lived happily ever after.

Harriette Hoover Green

The tears rolled down her face like an unending waterfall. They were too plentiful to wipe away, she just let them flow, releasing the energy she had been holding throughout her entire body. The more the muscles relaxed, the more the tears flowed. She went from feeling sad, to feeling a release of tension, to feeling a sense of *this is good, tears are good.* And, with that thought, the tears subsided. She exhaled a large breath, and then another. She thought, *the last thing she wanted to do was leave this place,* but she must.

They would be taking his body to the morgue, a thought that made her sick. This room was needed for other procedures. She knew she couldn't have them take the body home to the house, which is what she wanted. In her vision, she would bathe the body, dress him in his favorite suit and stretch him out on the living room sofa, the same sofa he grew up with from his family home in Chicago. But that, of course, would not be possible. Taking a body home is just not done today.

She needed to keep this job; trying to go against protocol may cause her bosses to think she was not capable of keeping her job. She sighed, wiped her face and stood up straight, ready to face the people on the other side of the door. She would be fine, she would be fine, she would be fine, kept running through her mind, as if repeating the phase would make it true.

When she entered the room with her bosses, her children, and his children, she promised herself she would not let them see her cry. Everyone hugged her and of course, the tears flowed again, but it was fine; it was tears all around. Crying together was a bonding experience that eased the pain each felt in their hearts.

She was so grateful to have had these 20 years together. Mack was the love of her life, he was her soul mate. She said, "We were all very lucky to have had Mack for all these years. Let us be grateful and not mourn his death. Remember Mack lives in each one of us through our memories. Every time we think of him, he is alive! Let us hold onto that thought, every day, every night." Brave words, easy to say; she would discover, not easy to do.

As she drove home she was in a fog, driving by instinct. The girls were taken home by their older siblings, who were then going on to their own homes. I think everyone wanted to be alone to allow the immensity of the reality of their own individual loss. She, her husband, the girls, their father, his son, the father he so loved, Mack was the most important person in the world to each of them.

At some point she had an image of losing both legs; being cut in half at the waist. Then the thought, *how can I live without my lower half?* However, could she do that? She was capable of managing on her own and did much of the time while Mack was away for a week or more before coming home. But he called every night when he was away to check in, to tell her he loved her and the girls, to hear what went on that day, and report the events of his day. They were a team. Now she would need to do it all on her own. Thank God she had taken the job here in the town where they lived; she would be close to the girls even when at work. That was a blessing!

Once alone in her room, the tears flowed again. The emotions were just too big to contain without sound or action, but she knew the girls could hear her if she screamed. She put her face into a pillow and released the moan she had stifled all day. She screamed and screamed until no sound came out and she was spent.

Splashing cold water on her face and holding a cold cloth to her eyes improved her appearance, but one could still see she had been crying. She went into the kitchen to prepare dinner. The girls were upstairs in their rooms. She prepared something quick and simple and called for the girls. They responded saying they would be down later. She ate a few bites and went to bed. This was the beginning of their disconnect, the girls and she. The loss was too great to bear. The reality of him never walking through the front door again, no more telephone calls with the beautiful resonance of his voice, deep, strong, reassuring and filled with love. Never to hold him again, make love with him again, laugh together, fight together, plan together, sleep together ever again. Gone without warning, forever. She could not bear it, but... she must.

As she lay there, her mind went back to the hospital, and over the events of the day, when she was told that Mack was in the hospital. She was sure he would be fine; after all he had survived two prior heart attacks. As they walked the short distance from her office in the Mental Health division of the hospital to the ER, her managers acted odd. There were no reassuring comments, no attempts to cheer her. Suddenly she thought, *He is dead. No! I would know if he was dead. I would feel it. I had no intuition of him even being in trouble.*

Once at the hospital she and her bosses were shown into a chapel type room, off the emergency entrance. This is when the doctor came in and told her they had worked on him for 3 hours, but could not get a sinus rhythm. Her mind didn't even protest, she didn't even protest, *but I was just 500 ft away; why didn't you find me? I work here!*

She asked to see him and was taken alone into an adjoining room. There he was, her Mack lying on the gurney, totally lifeless, clearly dead, cold to the touch. Even still *he was her Mack*. Later she wished she had stayed with him longer, climbed onto the gurney and lay with him. She never wanted to leave him; the last thing she wanted to do was leave this place where he was, but...

People always say to *live in the now*, that is all she could do. Thinking about the past was too painful, and thinking of the future was even more painful. No more famous Mackenzie hugs, no more Mack jokes, smiles, twinkling eyes, the sweet smell of his cologne, no more love making, no more dreaming of the future when it would be just the two of them. No future, period. Suddenly, she realized Mack existed in every cell of her being, however could she live without him? She realized she couldn't. She realized she was also, dead. She died when he died. She was dead inside. He was her world. He was the center of her universe. As much as she loved her children, all things always revolved around Mack. He was the first person to ever want whatever she wanted. He wanted what was best for her. He put her first, wanted her happiness first, assured she established a credit rating, assured she was able to finish her degree, arranged the wedding where she wanted. Did it her way. His was an unconditional love. He was her father, mother, mentor, best friend, lover, husband!

As the weeks turned into months, life became a routine with school events, concerts, football games with the girls in the band, or a play, or going to a dance. There were some happy times, but always missing Mack's presence. The months became years, two in fact, when she decided she wanted to live again! Really live. She needed to move on. The girls grew into teens and were dating. Their grief was equal to hers, but together they each moved on, slowly, slowly.

She decided she needed to go back to school to obtain her Master's Degree in Couples and Family Therapy, instead of the planned doctorate in Psychology. Tomorrow she would call and get registered for the next term. She could again read and retain information, after it being gone for many months. She could get through a day without crying and was again able to sleep several hours in a row before waking and lying there missing him. She could remember the past and enjoy the memories. She realized there actually is a future without Mack.

She is now living in Bend, Oregon.

KEVIN O'GRADY

Monty sat on the edge of the cliff. "I've never been more ready," he said, turning to Maria. Below him was a 1,000-foot drop that first fell straight down the sheer face of the granite cliff-face, and about the half-way mark it jutted out across several jagged outcrops with more sheer drop-offs, eventually leveling out into the glacial valley below.

Monty had been training for this for years. He started as a sky diver and when the cost of hiring airplanes and paying flying fees became too much, he turned to nature where the thrills and spins of tarp-flying or cloak-flying were free. He knew the dangers, but he knew the excitement was more than the dangers.

Maria stood with her back to him. Despite having been with him for ten years of his most dangerous jumps, she just could not stomach the sight of him jumping off such a steep cliff with not much protection other than a cape.

"I'm ready!" Monty said, excited to be one of the few to have tackled this particular jump, at this angle, at this time of the year. The updrafts changed at different times of the day and at different times of the year. But the updraft was perfect right now. Everything, including his whole life, was perfect right now.

Monty was thrilled that video technology had caught up with his sport, and he made one final adjustment to the GoPro camera on his helmet. Maria was not even a spectator to the dive, the footage from the camera was the only way she would participate. It was later in the tavern down at the trailhead 8 miles away that she would watch the death-defying dive.

She checked her watch and set her timer. The conditions were perfect for Monty, but not for her. She felt the fear rise up her back, standing the hair on-end on her neck. Despite the warm updrafts the fear always felt cold, and she wrapped herself in her poncho to prepare for her own descent down the trail to the tavern.

The excited scream from behind her was the only evidence she ever had that he had jumped. She never looked behind her. She never went to the cliff edge to see her lover fly past the eagles nests at high speed, or navigate the air currents as they flapped against his makeshift wings of cloth.

"He never came down," she sobbed. "He never landed where he should have. He must have hit something on the way." She was standing at the door of the tavern with her poncho wrapped around her. After several hours of waiting, the shock was beginning to have its effect, and she began to slowly accept the inevitable.

Search teams from the tavern and the local village had crawled the area on foot, the mountain rescue teams had flown over Monty's flight path in the Search and Rescue helicopter, but there was no trace of Monty.

As darkness descended on the valley, Maria found herself not accepting any offers of help. *The last thing she wanted to do was leave this place.* "Come home with us," they pleaded, but all to no avail. Maria was not moving. Minutes dragged into hours and the light faded fast.

Maria sat on the edge of the balcony of the mountain cabin, never taking her eyes from the tree line where her Monty was supposed to come down. The entire village had taken on a shocked silence. It was always the same when one of their own died in the pursuit of their sport. They feel the pain, they recall the excitement and the dangers in the pubs for several nights after the event, and then they go right back up there again.

Maria was sure she saw a movement from the edge of the pine trees. Her keen eyes were well adjusted to the terrain and the conditions from many years of camping and exploring in the outbacks of the most hostile terrain on earth. This time, she knew her eyes were not tricking her. She could make out the size and shape of Monty's body emerging from the undergrowth.

Maria ran down the steps and across the grounds of the tavern towards the trailhead. She tripped over several broken branches, and caught her poncho in the jagged edge of a broken aspen tree. She felt blood seeping from a cut over her eye as she floundered through the rocks to get to where she was sure Monty stood.

"Monty," she called. "It's me, Maria. Can you hear me?"

But there was silence. Only the gentle night breezes flapping the spring leaves spoke to her from the forest. She stopped and listened again, this time realizing that it might have been her own imagination that had tricked her. She was aware of how the mind can lead an unwary traveler to certain death in these parts. She knew too, that her expectation was being tested. She was recreating the joy of seeing him emerge from the trees like she had done so many times before. But he didn't emerge. Instead, she heard his whispering come across the gentle breeze.

She heard him clearly say, "You must leave this place and leave my memories here. I am where I always wanted to be, in the mountains."

An owl flew close to her, startling her. It was so silent in its flight that it was only Monty's guidance that had trained her to identify them in the darkness. She felt the rush of air against her face, and she knew it must be Monty. "I will search until I find you Monty, and only then will I leave this place."

The long white limousine pulled up in front of the Magic Castle in Hollywood. Nicole had always wanted to go there, but never dreamed of arriving in such luxury. Sam loved to spoil her and wanted this evening to be extra special.

The four passengers exited the hired car, all decked out in their finest; suits for the guys and long dresses for the ladies. Tonight, Sam and Nicole were celebrating their engagement with their best friends, Ron and Nancy. Fortunately, Ron was not only a magician, he was also a member of the Magic Castle, which entitled him to bring guests.

After dinner, the foursome headed to one of the magic shows where Nicole was pleased to be chosen as an assistant on stage. Normally, she was never in the spotlight. It was Sam who was a well-known Gospel singer, and usually the center of attention.

At one point they stopped by the bar. Ron wanted the others to experience the piano that magically played musical responses to people's questions. It was magical because no one was sitting at the piano, yet the keys moved as if someone were playing.

The minute Sam entered the room, the piano started playing his signature song, *How Great Thou Art*, which he sang at all his concerts. The four looked at each other in disbelief.

How did *Erma* the piano know who he was? Sam accused Ron of setting him up, which Ron quickly denied. Regardless, it all added to the fun.

Sadly, Nicole knew that the evening was coming to a close. *The last thing she wanted to do was leave this place.* They all shared some disappointment at having to end their time together. Then, Sam asked, "Why end it now? How about stopping at an after-hours club before heading back home?"

The limo driver took them past several places in the area, but nothing appealed to them.

Teasingly, Nicole mentioned that in about five hours the Sunday brunch at Caesar's Palace in Las Vegas would be open.

"Hey," said Sam, "that's not a bad idea!"

"I was only kidding," protested Nicole.

Sam asked the group, "What do you say? Breakfast at Caesar's Palace? After all, it kind of goes with an evening at the Magic Castle."

It was so like this man who loved living life in a large way. Fortunately, he had the money to do such a crazy thing. Without hesitation, Sam asked Danny, the limo driver, if he would drive them to Las Vegas. The poor guy looked a bit overwhelmed as he explained that this was the first time he had driven for the limousine company, so he'd have to call his boss.

Soon, permission was given and off they went. All four passengers napped throughout the three-and-a-half hour drive. When they got to Caesar's Palace, Sam gave Danny some money to get something to eat and asked him to return for them in two hours.

As they enjoyed brunch, Sam began thinking of the long ride back to Los Angeles, and the fact that their driver had been up all night, so he suggested that they all stay over night to relax and enjoy the day. When Danny returned to pick them up after breakfast, Sam gave him more money to go get a room for the night.

The next morning, when Danny picked them up, Nicole wondered what he must be thinking. Here they were, four grown-ups in clothes they'd had on for almost two full days, while holding four large stuffed animals that they had won at the Arcade in *Circus, Circus*.

True to his nature, as they headed back to Los Angeles, Sam suddenly asked the driver to take them by Hoover Dam, which was only a few miles out of their way. When the car pulled up in the parking lot, everyone piled out to look over the edge of the magnificent dam. However, it was so hot that the sightseeing was short-lived. By now the guys had shed their suit coats and the ladies were grateful that their long dresses were sleeveless.

Leaving the dam, they passed a small café that boasted a sign, *The Best Little Restaurant By A Dam Site.* They were laughing about the clever sign when Sam asked the driver to pull into a drive-through hamburger joint. Happy to get something to eat before the drive home, everyone placed their order. Then, as if someone was pulling a prank, the limousine made a strange sound and went silent.

Danny tried and tried, but couldn't get it started again. Finally, the guys had to push the limo out of the driveway so others could use the drive-through. Danny called for a tow truck, which had to come from Las Vegas. After a bit of a wait, finally a bright yellow tow truck pulled up to tow the limo back to Vegas. Stuffed into the back seat of the crew cab, hot and sweaty, and still carrying four stuffed animals, with a long white limousine following from behind, Nancy sighed and said, "And we didn't bring the camera!"

Ron, who was always joking around, said, "Now this is the way to go to Vegas! Anyone can rent a limo, but a limo and a tow truck?"

Nancy added, "Yea, this way we don't put so many miles on the limo!"

Traveling down the long stretch of desert highway, the humorous scene prompted the foursome to break into song as if on cue:

"Oh, we ain't got a barrel of money, maybe we're ragged and funny, but we'll travel along, singing a song, side by side."

A POEM BY DELL BLACKMAN

Be Sure To Share

Listen closely,
it's playing right now
There, right there
Can you hear it
Can you hear ...
the song of your life
the hymn of your soul
Listen again,
this time
with your heart
Much better now,
yes
What's that ...
you are the song
Right you are
Now,
sing your truth
and, share
always be sure
to share.

Prompt #14

They'll Float Too

AINGEAL ROSE O'GRADY

Abby looked at the short red dress hanging in her closet. She hadn't worn it in ages, yet it was the perfect choice for today's event. Her large brimmed sun hat with a ring of multicolored flowers around it was the perfect complement.

Today was the day for the annual sailing ships to pass through the harbor. It was always a gala event, but Abby hadn't made it the past couple of years due to other priorities. Abby's favorite part of this event was the myriad of brightly colored flags that blew so freely in the open air as well as the finely polished woods on board the various ships.

Abby often wondered what a journey on a sailing ship would be like, but she always came to the conclusion that it wouldn't be as romantic as she had imagined.

This day was special, more special than any of the other yearly arrivals of the sailing ships. Today Abby would meet Captain Anthony Bartholomew, the man who had been her pen pal since she was 19 years old.

Captain Bartholomew was 20 years her senior, but even so, the excitement running through her was as if she had been waiting for her long lost love to return home after lifetimes of being apart.

It was a perfect day. The sun was bright and warm and the sea was glistening with white sparkles that flashed on and off in random harmony.

Abby ran to the docks as the ships came in one by one. She was looking for one particular ship — *The Dawn's Light*. The stream of ships slowly came in one after the other, but *The Dawn's Light* was nowhere in sight. Abby began to panic. Her rush of excitement was now turning into waves of fear and she could feel the pounding in her heart increase moment by moment. Was this all a dream? Had she only imagined that Captain Anthony Bartholomew would really plan on meeting her in person after 20 years of correspondence on paper? She had never seen a picture of him, nor had she heard the sound of his voice. All she knew of him was his handwriting and it was the melody in his written words that had made her love him. Once he had sent her a gift of tiny dolphins carved out of a type of stone found only off the coast of Africa. He had only added a small note attached saying, *They'll float too*! *Love, Anthony*

Abby no longer stood along the docks waiting for Anthony. She had moved her shaking body to a large black boulder which had settled itself in the grassy area near the water.

She watched as village people and tourists made their way on and off the ten sailing ships anchored in the harbor. As noon approached, Abby solemnly began to walk back to her home. Dark thoughts filled her mind. The rejection was too much.

Upon arriving at her home a blue note hanging by a brown string swung merrily on her doorknob. The note said, "Twenty years is a long time to wait..." Abby thought the worst. Captain Anthony Bartholomew had moved on with his life... but then she felt someones arms caress her from behind. Captain Anthony Bartholomew whispered in her ear, ..."But wait I have!"

She turned to see his smiling face and in that moment, an eternity of distance dissolved into one divine embrace. They were finally home.

Once in grade school during recess, Jack Wilhelmy and I were playing on the swinging bar with our red-headed classmate Jimmy Hingston, when Jimmy flew off the bar and fell onto the dirt with an uncontrolled flapping about of his arms and legs. As Jimmy was getting up and brushing himself off, Jack said, "Don't worry! You can throw an Irishman into the sea."

As I was trying to parse that obscure statement into a meaningful thought, our games were interrupted by the school bell and we all headed back to our classrooms. I worked on that ethnic slur in my sixth-grade brain for the next hour. Was this German kid just making fun of our Irish friend because of his hilarious airborne antics, or was it something more profound about Irishmen?

My father's mother was born a Rowley from Rooney and was pure Irish, so I am a quarter Irish. Was a quarter of me being threatened with being thrown into the sea? What would I do if I were thrown into the sea? Would the sharks instantly eat me up, because of my Irish-ness, or was the statement a comment on the resiliency of Irishmen and no matter what happened to them they would cope with it with a characteristic comic aplomb?

My ten-year old brain was confused and now seventy-two years later that unforgettable statement still confuses me. Even Google failed me. Google usually comes up with millions of answers in an instant, but in this case it hadn't a relevant clue. *Will Irishmen float better than other people? Or what?*

I had that idea in my mind while out in San Francisco Bay in my kayak during a heavy storm, returning from where I had been searching for Sir Francis Drake's buried treasure. The waves were so high that when in a trough I couldn't see over them to the horizon and when on top there was a dangerously stiff wind. Would I cope with a capsizing? If Irishmen could be thrown into the sea and float, would it be enough to buoy up my English mitochondrial heritage and my doughty male Dutch ancestry too, both of which had some extensive nautical experience? I'm probably okay there, but my German ancestors made a quick voyage as paying passengers so probably that would lead to my sinking if thrown into the sea. I can't imagine anyone saying you can throw a German into the sea. Well, I suppose some other people can.

They'll probably float okay, but it's only part of all my heritage. I have some distant Dutch Astor relatives that went down on the Titanic and some from my

German side, too. They were totally unknown to each other. Some of them being of the very richest class and the others were either steerage or servants. But, no matter, the ice-cold Atlantic water swallowed them all.

Neither of these two groups of my distant relatives were Irish. Perhaps, if they had had a little Irish in them, like I do, they would have floated too. If Jack was right, you can throw an Irishman into the sea. *They'll float too*!

HARRIETTE HOOVER GREEN

It is a beautiful morning, gentle, quiet, soft. I actually feel good, I think I will be okay, at least for today, at least for a while. Opening the blinds increased the good feeling. Hmmm maybe I'm on the other side of the losses; the other side of the sadness.

As I went about my morning tasks the telephone rang. "Hello, how are you doing today?" the voice asked.

"Really good today, thanks for asking."

Silence. Is he waiting for details? Do I go on to share how bad it has been? How much do people really want to know about how I am doing? The voice proceeded to explain what he had been doing that week, then assures he has been thinking of me and missed me at a gathering I usually attend. *What a good friend.*

In a sudden decision, I heard my voice sharing the degree of distress I had been experiencing, culminating in my saying, "I'm not suicidal, but if I were, this past week I would have ended my life."

I then went on to explain the degree of physical pain, mental confusion, and memory blanks, the incidents of near catastrophes, and the sadness and loneliness that took me down, down, down as low as I've been since my husband, Mack, died many years before. Down, all the way to the bottom of the pit, feeling the pressure and weight of the earth covering me, struggling to breath. I had laid for hours and hours this week, rather than weeks, as I did after Mack's death!

In those days past, nearly 30 years ago, I would awake, forgetting he was gone. At other times, I would awake totally aware of his death and would be unable to open my eyes for what seemed like an endless amount of time. Once I opened my eyes, I would be unable to lift my head from the pillow.

Slowly, slowly the entire memory of his death would come into my awareness and the sadness would hit me like an avalanche of pain with a waterfall of tears. Sometimes, I would expel air and sound together clearly expressing the degree of agony I felt at the loss — aughhhhhhh. Then I would cover my mouth to prevent the sound from my children's ears; they hated it when I cried.

But today was a good day and this loss not as devastating. Having walked the path of loss in the past, one finds tools to help through the miles and miles, and hours and hours of sadness, anger, denial, and bargaining before acceptance would come, and go. Then there would be another round of all those emotions, just to come back to acceptance, before it would slip away again, and again. There will be a day of recognition and a sort of acceptance. Maybe today is that day.

Sometimes I would distract myself with tasks to avoid thinking about all that I no longer have in my life. Sometimes I would let the tears flow silently, absorbing into my entire being, mind, body, heart and soul the amount of love that generates such sadness. This current compounded loss is not so hard for many reasons, mostly because it was not a total surprise.

Today I have perspective and clarity about the losses, and a new life to create. The past loss offered only black, emptiness, hopelessness, just marking time. Breathing in and exhaling the pain, waiting for the day to end and another to pass, and eventually the girls will leave home and I can just howl my feelings into the universe.

Today I do not distract, I take the journey into the pain and into the loss, feeling it and allowing it to wash over me. I am not sure what set of circumstances triggered the depth of despair I experienced last weekend. Perhaps the recognition of the damage to my body and brain, which I have worked so hard to keep healthy and strong, now prevents me from living a normal life. The years and hours of aerobics and weightlifting lost due to the most recent rear end accident; the eighth. The recognition that at least 5 of those accidents caused whip lash and brain concussions and eventually, vertigo.

The most recent rear-end accident was such a small crash by comparison, yet to my body it felt huge. Immediate pain in my neck and back as experienced in all the prior crashes, big or small. It is good to understand that the cumulative damage is irreversible. It is helpful to now understand the totality of the challenges, cause of the vertigo and balance difficulties, memory lapses, anxiety and returned symptoms of PTSD (Post Traumatic Stress Disorder) are all related to the most recent accident. And, it is understood that any significant stressor can trigger the symptoms flooding back in altogether, overwhelmingly. The cause of the severe headaches, is still unknown, but once it comes, so comes the slide into depression.

But, all is well; there is a cure for the funky mood. I am so fortunate to be able to regain my center in heart, mind and soul. Being in my home, in the great room and looking out the huge windows at the sky, trees, bushes, architecture of the house next door, or watching the hungry ducks newly returned this spring with their ducklings looking for food. I did not see them mate this spring, but I have in the past. It will be such a joy to see the baby ducks who they will bring to the pond to eat and swim. *They'll float, too*, with mommy and daddy duck! Life is brightened by the regeneration of the cycles of the year, of the generations and the cycles of our lives.

There must be meaning in all the loss and all the pain. It certainly heightens the enjoyment of peaceful moments, times of shear joy, the beauty in nature and humanity, creating a depth of appreciation for it all.

All things are perfect, just the way they are is my belief, my knowing, the core of what I live by. This knowing deep in my being comes from the culmination of all my many, many lives. My belief is that over the endless number of lives I've lived, it all balances out. Life is ongoing. The lessons learned in this life will transport into the next life and the next. Any pain now teaches both now and in the future, allowing for growth, transmutation and evolution.

KEVIN O'GRADY

Mark filed the lawsuit the way he always did, fast and with venom. The court clerk's agent looked through it on the spot and quickly approved it. Mark sat back on the old wooden bench at the front of the empty courtroom. He rubbed his hands together with glee but quickly became aware of the clerk staring at him. He stopped in case any action he made might cause the District Court clerk to withdraw the document.

It had happened to him before when the clerk of the court had decided his case was vindictive. But this one would go all the way, and he would retire on the proceeds of the lawsuit. But he needed some inside help to ensure his plan would work. His thoughts went forward in time to Judge Corrigans ruling. He could hear the old judge say, "I award Mark McGregor the sum of 10.5 Million Pounds Sterling as compensation for the damages incurred through the failure of the defendant to act in a timely and appropriate manner, causing willful and indiscriminate loss of income to the plaintiff."

Judge Corrigan was getting on in years. He stood by the pond in the Botanical Gardens that had more or less grown around the courthouse since 1862. He needed to visit the gardens often to recoup his energy and to avoid the condemnation of the victims of his sometimes irrational rulings. He found it was the only way to stay clear-headed in the high-tension turmoil of the legal system.

Mark sat on the park bench to his right. He watched the old judge throw pebbles in the water, fooling the ducks into thinking it was food. Seagulls came screaming in to chase away the ducks and Mark could almost hear the old man's thoughts.

This is just like the courtroom. They scramble with greed for every scrap and morsel doled out by the judiciary. They are the gougers of the earth. They are the dregs of society. And I judge them accordingly.

Mark timed his approach. He didn't want it to seem contrived or threatening in any way.

"Beautiful day," Mark said casually.

"Ah, yes. It is wonderful to watch the balance of nature."

There was a dead silence between them for a few moments. Mark was anxious to make a good impression and he knew he only had this one shot at it. He was about to say, "Do you come here often," but decided that would not seem sincere, then it just blurted out. Mark was embarrassed by his sudden, unprofessional loss of composure.

"Yes, as a matter of fact, I do," the judge said with a slight smirk on his face. "I come here all the time. It keeps me sane in an insane world."

"I'm sorry," said Mark. "That was an adolescent thing for me to ask."

"Not at all. It is as good as anything between strangers." The judge was not giving much away.

Mark wondered whether to mention his case. *Not now,* he thought. *He doesn't know that I know he's a judge.*

"I've just come from the courthouse," Mark offered. The judge knew this too. Most people under pressure from the court system come into the gardens to pray.

"Yes, I meet many people here who are victims of all kinds of things. I meet the perpetrators too, and sometimes offer them advice, but mostly I stay out of their affairs. They come in here for forgiveness because they don't get it in there." As he said it, the judge flicked his eyes with disdain toward the courthouse and with that gesture, Mark seized his opportunity.

"Do you think I could ask your advice about something?" Mark had worked his scam successfully for so many years that he had developed the skills of a master manipulator. "I need help to dispose of some money."

Looking around for anyone or anything that might compromise him, and finding it clear, the judge said slowly and cautiously, "How much are you talking about?"

"About 10 million."

"Well, you could throw the notes in the pond. *They'll float too.*"

Mark decided to try another tack. The judge was way too experienced for this. "Do you have any children?"

"Yes, I have two girls. One is coming to Edinburgh next week to be married in our home parish, but I am having difficulty gathering her dowry in time."

Ah, the chink in the armor. Exactly what I need, thought Mark. "Maybe I can help. I am expecting a settlement from that same court over there. I can lend you some." Mark waited, knowing not to utter another word.

The judge threw another stone in the water. "Stones don't float, you know." Mark wondered why the judge would say something as stupid as that, especially when the moment was right to solve both their problems in a single stroke.

"But the notes would float. You said so yourself, and they would float right to your daughter. She would be very happy about that."

The judge looked out over the packed courtroom. He looked across at the plaintiff and noted how sorrowful and aggrieved he looked. His daughter's wedding was in two days and he would not have to do this dreadful work again. He paused, then, with his familiar authority, he said, "I am taking this opportunity to announce my retirement. I have spent 48 years on the bench maintaining justice in this country. This is my last ruling. Would the defendant please rise?"

The courtroom went silent. Mark swallowed hard. The judge announced his verdict.

Floating on the airbed in the pool of the Island resort of Las Palma, Mark saw a crisp, new 100-Pound Sterling note floating on the water beside him. Then a popping sound, and all the air left. His life support was gone.

LINDA KAY

How in the world would masquerading as a summer camp counselor fool any of her young charges, wondered Jenny? Camp Crystal Lake had a sterling reputation for being the best camp in the state, however, the recent rash of burglaries was cause for concern. They needed someone like Jenny who had experience as a detective, while still looking young enough to fit in as a camp counselor. They were hopeful that she would be able to discover the mystery of all the burglaries.

The Camp Director introduced Jenny to his intern, Tod. They chatted long enough for her to find out that Tod was a senior in high school, and had worked at several camps in the area over the past three years.

"Today we're going to take some of the kids on a float trip down the river on inner tubes," explained Jenny. "Please make sure everyone leaves cellphones and other valuables in their cabins. All they need is their bathing suits, a tee shirt and some type of hat. Oh, and remind them to put on lots of sunscreen."

The river flowed gently past the campgrounds, which was perfect for floating. There was just one small area where the river picked up a little speed as it flowed around a bend that constricted the flow of the water, however, it had always been easy to navigate.

After giving last minute instructions to the group, Jenny and Tod secured a net over a large inner tube and set the food and drink coolers inside so that they would not fall through. He quietly asked, "Is Butch Nelson, going with us? He seems to be sort of a troublemaker. He knocked down a bee hive last week, and some of the kids got stung. There's also been rumors of some things missing around here."

"Sounds like some unfortunate circumstances," she replied. "I'm sure everything will be fine."

Jenny stayed in front of the group. Tod was to follow up in the rear. Shortly after starting down the river, Butch decided to take off his life vest so that he could pull off his tee shirt. About that same time, the inner tube holding the coolers floated by. He could see that it was not attached to any other inner tubes, so he stretched out as far as he could to grab it as it floated past him. In so doing, he turned over his own inner tube and struggled to grab it before it floated off without him.

Without a life vest, and being close to the *food tube*, as the kids called it, he grabbed the rope that was dangling from its side. With that, the inner tube flipped over and down the river went the coolers.

Butch was able to hang on and kick his way to shore, but the coolers were long gone. Jenny missed Butch's fiasco since she was distracted by the sound of rushing water. She figured that they must be getting close to the bend in the river. As soon as she caught sight of the "little rapids," Jenny realized they were not so little. She was not about to take the group through such strong, rushing water, so she instructed them to quickly paddle to shore.

Once they got to shore, Jenny asked everyone to carry their inner tubes and walk along the river's edge until they got past the rapids.

Then she asked, "Where is Tod?"

"Don't know," answered one of the kids.

Just then Jenny spotted Butch slowly walking along the edge of the river just above them, struggling to pull the two coolers while an inner tube was perched over his head and under one arm. "I found the coolers," called Butch. "Should have known *they'll float too!*"

How in the world did he find them, she wondered? Relieved to see Butch and the coolers, she said, "Let's hurry and get back down to our pick-up spot. We can eat later."

Everyone got back in the water just past the ominous bend in the river. Arriving at their pick-up point for a ride back to camp, there was Tod. He had ridden down from camp with one of the pickup trucks that came to get the inner tubes.

"Where were you?", asked Jenny.

"Just as we were about to leave camp the director called to say my brother was on the phone. I figured I could catch up with you, but the call took longer than I thought," said Tod.

Jenny handed out sandwiches and soft drinks for the ride back to camp. The cook had told her there were two sandwiches for each person, and yet she was coming up short, so she passed on having something.

Back at camp, after dinner that night, the Camp Director called Jenny into his office. "I noticed that the Nelson boy, Butch, wasn't at dinner," he said. "Do you know why?"

"Butch confided to me that he helped himself to several sandwiches when he found the coolers this afternoon, and he was too full to eat dinner. I gave him the okay to return to his cabin," said Jenny.

"Well, evidently, there are some things missing from some of the cabins. What do you think we should do? What about talking to Butch?"

"I don't think that will be necessary," said Jenny, "actually, I think I have a good idea who our thief might be. Come with me while I talk to him so I have a witness."

Sitting across from Tod, and staring into a footlocker full of cellphones, money and other treasures, Jenny asked if he had anything to say.

"Nope," responded Tod. "I guess I shouldn't have lied about my brother calling."

"That was your first mistake," said Jenny. "Having already done a background check, I knew you didn't have a brother. Then you mentioned you had worked at several other camps in the past few years; each having had issues with theft. Grab your personal belongings, you're coming with me."

A POEM BY DELL BLACKMAN

The Backyard Of Home

They come before you now
as ancient from long ago
Pillars of love in the night ...
they're here to help you grow
Pealing away the shadows,
they're ancestors of the light
Sharing a love that shortens
any dim and distant sight
Peering through
that mirror of dreams ...
you will see more
than there seems
You will widen your glance
and come to know ...
these visitors are nothing if not
memories of your soul
Freeing you to run and roam
as the child that you are
in the backyard of your home.

Prompt #15

As I Was Standing There, The Book Simply Fell Off The Shelf. What Could I Do But Pick It Up?

What are 'accidents' and what are 'messages' from the cosmos? Being a Tarot card reader for over 40 years, there were many times when a client would shuffle the cards and one card would randomly jump out of the deck onto the table or floor. Clients always thought this was a meant-to-be card, although I never thought so. Then there were times when I would be walking down the street and a white feather would suddenly float down from out of nowhere and land on the sidewalk in front of me. On those occasions, I always thought that was a sign that someone from spirit was saying, "Hello." Those moments always occurred when I was feeling alone or going through some period of doubt in my life.

So, which events are 'accidents' and which are 'messages'? I know, for example, that the appearance of hawks on my fencepost or flying across my windshield while I'm driving my car are good omens for me. They let me know I'm on the right track in my life and that I'm being guided.

Other signals and omens such as receiving in the mail 'by accident' a decorator plate of two gray humpback whales right when I was trying to decide whether or not to go on a Caribbean boat trip to swim with those same whales was definitely a sign from spirit.

Another time I was frequenting my favorite local bookstore and I was perusing the aisles as I love to do. One book in particular had peaked my interest. *As I was standing there, the book simply fell off the shelf! What could I do but pick it up?* Curiosity made me glance at the title, *This is Your Life*. Ironically, it was in the Biography section, a section I would not normally be interested in. I took the book and sat down in a cozy chair at the far back of the book store and opened the front cover. The words, *This is Your Life* seemed to glare at me off the page. I was almost afraid to go any further. Was this some Twilight Zone event? Was I going to fall down the rabbit hole and be met by random mysterious creatures and events with no conscious control?

Watching the fear bubble up in me, I turned to the acknowledgement page. The book was dedicated to a litany of casts and characters — everyone *I* had ever met or encountered in my life, down to my pets, their offsprings, zoo animals, friends and relatives, teachers and the like! All were mentioned in chronological order, no one or thing was missing. After turning the many pages this covered, the next page simply said,

You have arrived, congratulations!

Where had I arrived? At that particular time in my life, I was feeling I had arrived nowhere. I was going through a period of no sense of direction, no urgings that lead anywhere in particular. What would the next page reveal? The next page simply said, *Here.*

Here – what a strange word. It almost annoyed me with its simplicity. *Here.* Okay I'm *here.* I looked around — what was around me? Shelves of books of all colors, descriptions, information, puzzles and stories ; a vast collection of choice. People walking by of equally diverse descriptions — male, female, short, tall, middle, children of all ages looking, enjoying and searching. But where was *I*? What was *I* doing? *I* was in the midst of life happening, being one of the many players in the scene, doing my own thing, playing the game with all the others.

Was this an 'accident'? I asked myself. Arriving here, watching the other players in the game of life. Was my ending up here meant to be or was it all a mistake?

There were still two other pages left in the book. I opened the next page and it read, *Welcome Home.* Now what did *that* mean? What is Home, and was this Home? This cozy chair, the bookstore, the people, books, toys, the café — was this Home?

I became suddenly aware that it was *all* meant to be. No accidents, no chance happenings. I was enveloped in love. All the players in the game loved me and I loved them.

We had all agreed to be here to support and show up for one another in the game of life. Each and every moment had been arranged, they for me, I for them — one movement.

I turned and opened the final page. It simply said, *Amen.* And there it was. I was with all the others in a living prayer called life.

CHARLES SCAMAHORN

As I was standing there, the book fell off the shelf. What could I do but pick it up? My reflex was to put it back where it came from on the third shelf at Dudley's Bookstore. That response comes from my self-training of sixty years to instantly do the right thing.

It was a New Year's resolution made in 1968 when I was studying Gurdjieff's (G) philosophy. At that time I was living in Berkeley, California, and my closest friends were from the Channing Club. That is a Unitarian college-age discussion group I had been a member of for several years at WSC. Most of these grad students were reading G's book, *All and Everything,* and participating in a separate discussion group where they practiced self-observation. I decided not to join that second group until I had read the book. That turned out to be a BIG mistake, because the book is almost impossible to read. The author G insists in the introduction that you be willing to read the book three times or put it down right away and walk away.

Because my friends spoke so highly of it I decided to read it the required three times. Big mistake! But it was a choice that made a huge impact on my life. G wrote that we should read the book the first time like we would read any other book, and that we should read it the second time out loud, like this post is designed to be read. We should only attempt to understand it on the third reading. The problem was, and it would still be a problem for any reader today, it is nearly impossible to read the first time.

Well, I did follow G's instructions, but it took me about six years to finish reading it the first time. It only took about two years to read it the second time, and two months to read it the third time. The reason it was so quick and easy to read the third time is easy to say but impossible for you to understand without reading it.

The book is a pure comedy on the third reading! It is filled with sarcasm, scorn and pity at the human situation. It isn't until the third reading that you realize you have been led down a path that seems perfectly logical and reasonable at first, but what is to be learned from each of the stories the third time is quite different from what was learned on the first reading.

On the first reading the people in the stories learned valuable life lessons and they applied those lessons to their daily lives. On first reading, these lessons are promoted as valuable wisdom. On the third reading, they are understood to be the wisdom of absolute fools.

Therein lies the comedy to be understood in the third reading, a sardonic comedy, and perhaps it could be thought of as a cruel comedy.

But one comes out of the whole process a sadder and a wiser person because you learn to see human foolishness more clearly. I never did join one of the G self-observation groups, but I feel that I am much better off for reading *All and Everything* three times as instructed and for not joining a group. It was my habit cultivated long ago to instantly do the right thing. And I reflexively stooped over and picked up the book and put it back on the shelf.

HARRIETTE HOOVER GREEN

There are a lot of ways to approach a dilemma; one can engage, ignore it or laugh it off, walk away or listen with your heart. Liz and I listened with our hearts to each other; she was my best friend. And, if she were to drop something, what could I do but pick it up! She would do the same for me. This just means we had each other's back, we would help in whatever way possible.

We met in a library looking at books in the same section. We were talking for the longest time, getting to know each other. *As I was standing there, the book simply fell off the shelf. What could I do but pick it up?* We looked at each other, both realizing this was a sign!

"What's the title?" Elizabeth asked?

"*The Prophet* by Kahlil Gibran," I said, as I opened the book to see what it was about. "It is obvious that we are meant to read this book — it almost fell on my foot. Is it okay if I check it out first and then you can check it out?" I asked. She agreed, explaining she was reading three books concurrently and could wait.

This is the first I've written about our adventures. I think this story will whet your appetite for more. The story begins when we met, but this is the story of our first adventure. I'll begin with our brief history and jump forward into the wilderness, where there is no judgment, no one to accuse you of wrongdoing and no one to praise you for being a hero. This is totally your own decision, yours and your conscience. What would you have done?

My friend Elizabeth (Liz for short, but only for this author's convenience), would never allow anyone to call her Liz. Anyway, Liz and I were off on an adventure driving to Washington D.C. and leaving eight children behind in the care of their father's and baby sitters. Granted, no one was a baby, although my youngest, my son Dirk, was only four years old. The husbands insisted we needed a break, Elizabeth more so than I. She had five sons and I had two daughters and a son. We both felt we needed a break from the endless questions of *why mommy* from the children. A break from the endless tasks of cooking, cleaning, dishes, laundry, managing the social calendar and family events like birthdays and holidays and of course, the marital bed duties. One could say the 'bloom was off the rose' of marriage, homemaking and sex.

Elizabeth said she didn't need a map to get to D.C., "We'll just follow the signs from one big city to another — it'll be fun," she said. "We'll follow our intuition." Well, we did know that Washington, D.C. was east of Michigan, but in truth, I didn't know for sure all the states in-between. But I was sure Elizabeth did. So, off we went without a map, and this is way before cell phones or GPS in your car.

Elizabeth was a bit of a rebel, very independent, very head strong and very smart. I'm sure she's the only Republican City Councilman's wife who had a 'Vote Democratic' sticker on her car! She was gorgeous with ginger red hair, 5'10", slim, even after having five boys. Every one's head would turn when she walked into a room. I felt like a little country mouse in her presence, but she always treated me as an equal. She once told me she liked how I also got attention when I walked into a room.

After driving all day, we discovered we were lost. It was now very dark. We were on a country road, no other cars, no lights, no signs. "We must have missed a sign back there," I said, sounding just a wee bit worried. "What direction does your intuition tell you to go?" I asked. "I think we should turn around," Liz said, "My sense is to continue forward. There is nothing back there but a lot of dark road for miles and miles!" was my response.

We had been talking about our lives, our beliefs and our marriages. The conversation was so intense we had paid no attention to the wide open, empty road. "Okay, we'll flip a coin, since we don't hold the same vision," I said. I didn't want to admit to her that

I didn't really think I had an intuition, but I did feel strongly that going forward was the right direction. So, we got out of the car to flip the quarter. When she flipped the quarter it went so high that we didn't see where it fell. "I think it rolled under the car," I said. As we were looking around under the car, we both heard a low rumbling. "Tell me that was thunder," I said. Liz said, very quietly, "Get in the car, *now*, it' a BEAR!" We scrambled into the car slamming the door behind us and locking all the doors. "Did you see a bear?" I asked, shaking. "No, but I heard a bear and it sounded really close," said Liz.

Liz put the car in gear and tore out of there like a bat out of hell! After a time we realized we were going forward and just kept going. The lights of the car picked up a highway sign — *Pennsylvania Border 50 Miles Ahead Toll Road.*

As we approached the toll booth, it was empty. No one was around, and there were no lights anywhere. Liz inched the car forward, slowly getting ready to pitch the $1.50 worth of coins into the overflowing basket with coins scattered all around the basket! As Liz prepared to toss our $1.50 into the overflowing basket, we were both struck by the same thought. "Wait!" we said in unison. We both recognized that we could (1) not put any money in the basket or (2) we could take the money! There was a lot of money there; it would sure add nicely to our very limited spending money!

What a moral dilemma! Taking the money would be stealing, whether anyone saw us or not. We are women of integrity, but who would know? Just us. Who would miss the money? How could it hurt? We sat there deep in thought, kind of hoping someone would come along so we'd no longer have a choice, but the road remained empty, totally black, no approaching headlights.

Suddenly Liz tossed our $1.50 in the bin. It bounced off, as if to say it was stupid to toss money into an overflowing bin that someone else could come by and take for themselves. I opened the car door — what could I do but pick it up?

Believe it or not, we made it to D.C. and drove right into Georgetown, the 'in' place to go, unbeknownst to us. We had adventures galore, beginning in Georgetown and later after dinner. The next day a policeman stopped us as we were strolling the city after having had dinner. He said, "Ladies, it is not safe for you to be walking unattended by a gentleman here in the city." We were both so surprised that we laughed and said, "It would be a sorry day for anyone to give us a bad time. Thank you officer for your concern, we can take care of ourselves." Oh, how I now realize how very, very naive we were, us little country bumpkins !

More adventures with Liz and I to come.

KEVIN O'GRADY

Constance stared at the bookshelf hoping for inspiration. Things had been happening too quickly lately for her to think clearly. The interim government forced her to go on the run and her husband had to escape to the islands.

As she stood alone in her luxury apartment on Mykonos, her mind raced to the first time she had arrived on the beautiful Greek island. The summer was over and the tourists had left, leaving behind a kind of blissful peacefulness that was celebrated by the locals in the Tavernas in dance and the smashing of plates. As she watched the ferry leave the small harbor, she wondered if her Greek husband had done the right thing by bringing her here.

She watched the locals feed the pelican they fondly called Petros. He had become their logo, their symbol for an ideal location to rest and recuperate in the warmth of the Mediterranean sunshine.

But it was also the name of the instigator of the riots, the one known as Petros the Pest.

Her attention ran to the string of events that found her here in this moment. The riots in the streets had begun with the story of a rich family embezzling government money for their own use to buy property on the islands. The island properties were becoming increasingly valuable due to the recent designation of the entire region as a Unesco area of outstanding natural beauty.

But it was becoming inflated too quickly and Constance could see the beginnings of high-rise apartments, big name hotels and cell towers already under construction along the oceanfront and by the tiny harbor.

She wondered why her husband kept his intentions from her, when her thoughts were suddenly shocked into the present moment by huge bronzed arms wrapping around her from behind.

"Yalla," he said warmly. "You will love it here." And then he paused and said, "For the moment." She loved his embraces. He was strong from being a fisherman all his life, but lately his government position as island liaison in the Department of Tourism had placed him in direct conflict with the money interests of huge corporations worldwide.

"Come," he said, taking her hand and walking briskly down the newly constructed walkway, past the million dollar yachts anchored in the new slipways that dominated the once peaceful island harbor scene. "Come, we must move quickly," he said.

She noticed the urgency in his voice. "What's going on?", she asked, worried that her preconceived idea of this being an island getaway was about to be shattered.

"I have a safe house on the other side of the island," he said. "Here, take this seat." He sat her on the back of the tiny speedboat and within minutes they were tying up by a small fishing cottage that sat at the end of a tiny slipway in the shelter of the south side of the island.

"I will be back in an hour," he said, and with that, he was gone. The half-door swayed gently in the warm Mediterranean breeze, and the smell of goat cheese wafted in the air.

"Hurry, come with me!", a voice said from behind a hand-made curtain that shielded the small kitchen from the living room. "Hurry." The voice was Greek, with the faintest hint of Italian.

Believing this to be part of her husband's plan, she went with the Greek into the back room where she stood beside an old wooden bookcase.

"How did you find me?", he asked. There was an urgency in his voice. A veiled threat.

Suddenly, there was a movement from the bookcase. A book fell from the middle shelf right at her feet. She caught a glimpse of a gun barrel poking through before she saw the flash of the gunshot.

Her reverie was cut short by her husband speaking to her from their new home in the penthouse in the newly constructed Holiday Harbor Suites on the island.

"The book of life worked," he said.

"The trap you set worked perfectly. *As I was standing there, the book simply fell off the shelf. What could I do, but pick it up?* And the shot went right past me and killed Petros."

LINDA KAY

My neighbor's father had passed away after a serious illness. Since my mother and neighbor had known each other for a long time, my parents and sister and I all attended the funeral. As everyone was standing around the grave site visiting, the neighbor told mom that she was concerned that some people planned to stop by her dad's house after the service and she'd had no time to buy food, or do the dishes, or straighten up the place.

Always wanting to be helpful, my parents offered to stop and pick up some food, and then asked my sister and me to drive over to the old man's house to help pick things up so it looked nice for visitors. Since we had never been there before, mom gave us some quick directions, while adding that it was easy to spot since it was painted a very bright blue. She also mentioned that it would be unlocked, so we wouldn't need a key.

My sister and I hurried across town and found the house. We knew there was little time before people would be showing up, so we did our best to rush in and make the bed and wash the few dishes in the sink. We were picking up some of the old newspapers that were piled around the living room, when I got distracted by the old man's collection of books. He had dozens of shelves built into the wall, and there had to be hundreds of books. Curious, I couldn't help but scan some of the titles.

One of the books caught my attention. I started to reach for it just as my cell phone rang. At the same moment, *as I was standing there, the book simply fell off the shelf. What could I do but pick it up?* It was titled, *Trespassing on Einstein's Lawn.* What a curious title I thought.

But before I could open it, I had to answer the phone.

I heard my mom's stressed voice on the other end asking, "Where are you? I thought you were coming to the house to help tidy it up!"

"We are at the house and we have been busy doing everything you asked us to do," I answered in total confusion.

"Well, I'm at the house and I don't see you or your sister; and nothing has been done! Are you sure you are on Elm Street?"

With that I raced out the front door to look at the street sign. "Yes," I assured her. "We're on Elm Street, and this is a bright blue house, and the front door was unlocked just like you said!"

The next thing I heard was my mother saying, "Oh, my goodness! Look down the block, there is another bright blue house at the end of the street. You are not at 369 Elm!"

I was almost afraid to look at the house numbers in front of me. "Yikes! Mom, you're right. We are at 361! It was bright blue just like you said, and no one was home, so we forgot to double check the house number."

The first thought was to leave before the people who lived there showed up. It was an awful feeling to realize we had been at some stranger's house making their bed and washing their dishes. However, my sister and I got about two doors down and then decided to go back to the house and at least leave a note so the residents would not wonder what happened, or worse, think that there may have been a burglary.

Deciding to turn our total embarrassment and fear of trespassing into a more positive experience, our note said: *While you were out, some good fairies came by to tidy up the house and surprise you. Please forgive us if we put something away in the wrong place, however, know our hearts were in the right place.*

A POEM BY DELL BLACKMAN

Sometimes

Sometimes ...
When paths cross upon the journey
Sometimes the ways of each will part
Sometimes something is left behind
Later, to be discovered in the heart.

Creative **BEND** *Writers*

Acknowledgments

The Bend Creative Writers Group is grateful for all the assistance received in the publication of this community book. We thank each of the contributing authors and their spouses for their generous support of each other, and especially for being so consistently positive and patient through each of our writing meetups.

Not all prompts originated from books, but for those that did, we acknowledge all those authors. We have mentioned as many of them as we could find in the Bibliography on the next page.

Clockwork Purple was part financially supported by Michael Murray, himself an author with several successful books under his belt. Anonymous donors helped through our crowdfunding campaign for which we are deeply grateful.

We are also grateful to Dudley's Bookshop Café in Bend, OR for their writing space and superb ambience. We thank the local newspapers and magazines for their support in helping launch the book, and we thank the Bend, Redmond, and Sisters bookshops for kindly stocking it for us.

We acknowledge Twin Flame Productions and their Harmony House imprint for their publishing expertise. Without their help, this book would not have been published. And finally, we thank you the reader, because you make it all worthwhile.

Bibliography

Prompt #1 — And Still There Is The Wonder — No source found.

Prompt #2 — Burned My Hand Badly While Holding A Red And Green Fire Cone — *Beautiful Losers* by Leonard Cohen Pg 63, Line 5 — http://amzn.to/2pXg9rM

Prompt #3 — Clockwork Purple — Bend Creative Writers. No source found.

Prompt #4 — For Eddie, Music Was More Than Just Sound — *Lakeshore Chronicles Series: Snowfall at Willow Lake* by Susan Wiggs — http://amzn.to/2rvkILb

Prompt #5 — He Took A Few Steps As If Walking Upright — *The Poet Prince*: A Novel by Kathleen McGowan — Pg 82, Line 3 — http://amzn.to/2q0wVoZ

Prompt #6 — I Couldn't Concentrate, My Thoughts Finned Off Into The Distance — No source found

Prompt #7 — I Had Come To NY To Try Something New — *Tune Smith* by Jimmy Webb, Pg 20, Line 9 — http://amzn.to/2pXDrO4

Prompt #8 — Just Who Will You Be? — *Big Question. Little Book. Answer Within* by Maria Shriver — http://amzn.to/2riwiMk

Prompt #9 — More Than One Winter Has Found Me Working In A Silver City Dive That Beckons To The Thirsty With A Classic Neon Sign Of A Cactus In The Foreground And A Horseman Drifting Alone Into The Distance — *Fire Season* by Philip Connors — http://amzn.to/2pXqrIr

Prompt #10 — Mysterious And Wondrous Ways In Which Libraries And Animals Enrich Humanity — *Dewey The Small-town Library Cat Who Touched the World* by Vicki Myron — http://amzn.to/2rvfj66

Prompt #11 — One Way Or The Other, That Gives Poetry Its Musical Qualities — *Tunesmith: Inside the Art of Songwriting* by Jimmy Webb — http://amzn.to/2pXDrO4

Prompt #12 — She Wanted This Couple To Be Comfortable, But More Importantly, She Wanted Them To Stay Long Enough For Them To Get All The Answers They Needed So Desperately — *The Reincarnation of Columbus: Coping with the Death of a Child from SIDS* by Kevin O'Grady — http://amzn.to/2rv1uVX

Prompt #13 — The Last Thing She Wanted To Do Was Leave This Place — No source found.

Prompt #14 — They'll Float Too — No source found.

Prompt #15 — As I Was Standing There, The Book Simply Fell Off The Shelf. What Could I Do But Pick It Up? — Charles Scamahorn

Creative BEND Writers

About The Authors

In the following pages, the authors are listed alphabetically by name.

Aingeal Rose O'Grady— Aingeal Rose is a prolific author of 13 books that bring readers peace, comfort and inspiration through her straight-forward and uniquely inspiring messages. She is an internationally known master reader and teacher of the Akashic Records. This ancient library is a database in spirit that answers life-changing questions from each individual's own record of their many lifetimes and sojourns in Spirit.

Trusted by clients around the world for her down to earth and authentic approach, Aingeal Rose effectively combines spiritual guidance and intuition with eye-opening readings of the Akashic Records freeing her clients from old beliefs that have held them hostage throughout their lifetimes. She has been accessing this incredible library for over 25 years and enjoys exploring life's deeper issues, including the purpose of life and why we are here. Aingeal draws on her inquisitive and intuitive nature while writing for *Clockwork Purple*!

Aingeal Rose can be contacted at http://aingealrose.com

Charles Scamahorn — I asked my garden gnome Samumpsycle, "What should I say about my life?" He implied, with his always inscrutable smile, "That's your problem, but never lie!" Hmm...

I've attempted to live a quiet life of always seeking defined low-stress ways to relate to the world but I crossed Joe McCarthy's hit-list by inviting J. Robert Oppenheimer to speak at my college. Then, I chose a quiet career as a pilot in the US Air Force, but Gen. Curtis Lemay disagreed with my decision as a B-47 pilot not to drop H-bombs on people, and he said 10-years in prison for me, but discharged me instead, and I found Berkeley. I lived there quietly for 50 years, always avoiding the riot police and once exiting the third story balcony of Sproul Hall on a rope to the cheers of thousands of people during the free-speech movement sit-in. I helped found the Berkeley Barb with Max Scherr and sold the first bundle of Barbs on the 2400 block of Telegraph Avenue. Most people find me boring, so I'm working on buffing my boring side with these short stories.

Contact Charles at https://probaway.wordpress.com

Dell Blackman — Dell Blackman is an intuitive poet who believes that life is all in the heart, and that our purpose is to live as soul. This native Oregonian has a special gift of simplifying the most thought-provoking ideas about life and living life's purpose, which is why he was invited to be a part of this publication.

In his own words, here are some thoughts from the poet: "There is a phrase, *we're all just walking each other home.* Well, on the way home, I've done a little exploring and I am just trying to share some discoveries I've stumbled upon. It is my intention to offer some thoughts, feelings, and perceptions that may inspire others to discover their own joy and truth in life. I want readers to experience the happiness of an open heart and to know love. In other words... themselves."

Dell's poems can be found on Facebook at https://www.facebook.com/dell.blackman

Harriette Hoover Green, A.K.A. M.Joanna White-Wolff's stories are thought-filled and engaging, reflecting her experience as a woman, and a psychotherapist who has been married, divorced and widowed. She had five children. Her prosaic writing style often mirrors her motto, which comes from that old song, *What Does Love Have To Do With It?* "EVERYTHING,"she says.

Her extensive professional background as a licensed psychotherapist had her working in the field for 30+ years blending old and new techniques wrapped around her spiritual beliefs.

Kevin O'Grady — In his first book, *The Reincarnation of Columbus*, Kevin shares his real-life journey in a gripping story of how he coped with the grief and loss of his first-born son. Born in Ireland and now living in Bend, Oregon, Kevin has the gift of expanding the mind and bringing wonder and awareness to those seeking spiritual empowerment. He is known to quickly ignite the spark of understanding in clients, students and readers, and he does it again in *Clockwork Purple*.

Whether you listen to him on his *HonestToGodSeries.com* podcasts, enjoy his visionary artwork, hire him for intuitive coaching, or read this book, you will be inspired and empowered.

Kevin can be contacted at https://ahonu.com or http://twinflameproductions.us

Creative  *Writers*

Linda Kay — Fiction devotees discover a refreshing simplicity in Linda's short stories, while being transported to memorable situations that offer an element of surprise. Linda Kay's writing career began by accident when asked to write a script for a television commercial to help her friend sell an idea to a new account. From there, she wrote copy for record album covers, brochures and magazine ads as part of her job as an advertising and marketing professional.

Before joining the *Bend Creative Writers* group, non-fiction had been her emphasis from editing newsletters to co-authoring the book, *Instant Feng Shui – Just Add Wind and Water*. You are invited to savor the magic Linda brings to the stories she shares. Linda's book can be found at http:// amzn.to/1UHMxKe

Creative BEND *Writers*

Bend Creative Writers are prolific. They found they had too many stories for their first published work *Clockwork Purple*, so they funneled the extra stories into Volume 2. Then they discovered they had enough for Volume 3, and so it went! You can find all the books on their website at:

https://clockworkpurple.com

Or, search on Amazon.com for the title, *Clockwork Purple*, or the name, Bend Creative Writers, or by ISBN:

Volume 1 — ISBN **978-1-880765-01-2**
Volume 2 — ISBN **978-1-880765-02-9**
Volume 3 — ISBN **978-1-880765-03-6**

Other books by the authors include:
A Time of Change by Aingeal Rose — http://atimeofchange.info
The Nature of Reality by Aingeal Rose & Ahonu — http://thenatureofreality.info
Answers From The Akashic Records by Aingeal Rose & Ahonu — http://answersfromtheakashicrecords.com
The Reincarnation of Columbus by Kevin O'Grady (Ahonu) — http://thereincarnationofcolumbus.com
Instant Feng Shui — Just Add Wind & Water by Linda Kay — http://amzn.to/1UHMxKe

Made in the USA
San Bernardino, CA
04 August 2017